Who could she possibly be?

Edging closer to the woman he'd just saved from drowning, Edward cradled her against his body. As he did so, he was struck by the purity of her features—eyes framed with thick, dark lashes, an aquiline nose and a full, rosebud-shaped mouth. She really was quite beautiful. She smelled of seawater and some exotic perfume, and her skin...

His heart made an odd sort of twisting sensation in his chest and he took a deep breath. As he did so, her eyes opened, and he found himself staring into irises black as midnight.

"Who—?" she breathed.

"Who am I?" Edward was used to dodging that question, but for the first time in years, he was tempted to tell the truth. *Tell her? And have her metamorphose into some sort of sycophant, or treat him with distant respect, like royalty?*

"I'm just an innocent bystander," he said, instead.

Her long lashes fluttered as she took in his wetsuit, his dripping hair.

"You...look...like...a frog...."

Dear Reader,

Once upon a time we were little girls dreaming of handsome princes on white chargers, of fairy godmothers who'd made us into beautiful princesses, and of mountain castles where we'd live happily ever after.

Now that we're all grown up, we can recapture those dreams in a brand-new miniseries, ONCE UPON A KISS. It features stories based on some of the world's best-loved fairy tales—expressly for the little girl who still lives on inside us.

Lisa Bingham continues the series with the retelling of the unique fairy tale *The Princess & the Frog*.

Be sure to read all six of these wonderful fairy tale romances, coming to you only from American Romance!

ONCE UPON A KISS—at the heart of every little girl's dreams...and every woman's fantasy....

Happy reading!

Debra Matteucci
Senior Editor & Editorial Coordinator
Harlequin Books
300 East 42nd Street
New York, NY 10017

Lisa Bingham

THE PRINCESS & THE FROG

Harlequin Books

TORONTO • NEW YORK • LONDON
AMSTERDAM • PARIS • SYDNEY • HAMBURG
STOCKHOLM • ATHENS • TOKYO • MILAN
MADRID • WARSAW • BUDAPEST • AUCKLAND

To Bonnie Crisalli,
Thanks

ISBN 0-373-16692-3

THE PRINCESS & THE FROG

Copyright © 1997 by Lisa Bingham Rampton.

Chapter One

Carrie Randall gripped the yacht's brilliant brass railing and squeezed her eyes shut. Maybe if she didn't look at the water, she wouldn't feel so...so...

Sick.

No. I can't throw up. Not here. Not now!

Her stomach roiled for several more seconds, then settled into a more tolerable ache. Thankful she had averted losing her lunch on the polished teak at her feet, Carrie quickly opened her eyes, seeking some other means to distract her thoughts from the nausea that had gripped her thirty minutes before she even arrived at the wharf.

She and water had never really taken to one another. One look at the dappled surface bobbing and dipping, and...

Don't think about it. Don't think about anything—or, if you must, keep your mind on something other than water.

Analee, Carrie decided fiercely. Analee Adler was responsible for Carrie's current plight. Analee knew very well that Carrie was prone to seasickness.

Hadn't Carrie's employer witnessed the phenomenon firsthand when she attempted to "treat" Carrie to a cruise? Carrie had spent the entire week comatose in a cabin the size of a broom closet, much to Analee's irritation.

Carrie fixed her gaze on the shiny brass doorknob three yards away. At least she'd had the good sense to abandon the other guests, who had gathered around the bar in the saloon. Out on the deck, she was alone in her agony. Well, nearly alone. Her only companion was another guest, an elderly woman who had come outside to read, and who looked suspiciously like Tweety's mistress. Her plump body had been wedged into an iron-control girdle and was swathed in a tailored rayon dress with an obnoxious geometric print. Her head, balanced upon a neck that was far too short, seemed pea-size in comparison to her body, and her steel gray hair had been pulled so tightly into a knot that her eyes appeared slightly crossed. As a final flourish, the woman had chosen a bright yellow pillbox hat. A ridiculously large silk poppy poked from the top, the brilliant scarlet petals flapping in the breeze as if the flower were some sort of bird, attempting to fly away.

Carrie's eyes fixed on the flower, as if it had some trancelike effect. *I know just how you feel, pal. I'd love to get off this barge, too.*

Barge.

Suddenly, the fluttering silk flower reminded Carrie all too clearly of the boat shifting beneath her, back and forth, back and forth.

Abruptly Carrie returned her attention to the doorknob, while inwardly she continued her lamentation. If only Analee hadn't insisted that Carrie journey to Babcock Island.

"I know I haven't officially been asked to the Babcock Gala, Carrie darling. But Sissy Munchausen received an invitation, passed on to her by her sorority sister, Bunny Wilkerson. Bunny couldn't go, due to her recovery from her latest face-lift. And when Sissy couldn't make the event, she said I could go in her place. You might have a bit of a tussle with Babcock's infamous security guards, until you explain the situation, but I know you'll be able to persuade them to let me attend. After all, I am Babcock Publishing's hottest author."

Evidently Edward Babcock hadn't thought the distinction that important, or he would have invited Analee in the first place, Carrie had thought cynically.

"In the meantime, see that my things arrive safely, Carrie dearest. I called my housekeeper with a list of antique gowns to pack in my hand-tooled leather luggage. I know the old dresses are actually yours, but since I allowed them to be shipped to my address, I figured you wouldn't mind if I borrowed them for a few weeks. Oh, and make sure my best gold-inlaid jewelry case is waiting for me when I arrive."

Sighing, Carrie wished with all her heart that

Analee had entrusted one of her other "grunts" with the task of guarding her jewelry. Analee became positively rabid if even one of her precious earrings fell to the floor. She rarely allowed Carrie to be in the room when the case was opened—as if she feared Carrie might have subversive connections with the Cat Burglars of America.

The boat rolled through a particularly high swell, and Carrie gripped the railing again. Why, *why,* had Analee done this to her? Was it a test of Carrie's loyalty and dependability? Or had the order been given out of premeditated cruelty? Without the jewelry case, Carrie could have taken a dose of medication. Failing that, she could have excused herself from the other passengers and spent the channel crossing in the privacy of the bathroom.

Or was it called the "head" at sea?

She sighed. It didn't really matter what that wonderful niche of privacy was called. Carrie wasn't about to visit a bathroom, a head, a loo or a water closet anytime soon. She knew from past experience that going belowdecks was the worse thing a seasick person could do. Ironic as it sounded, she'd been told that the best thing she could do was stand at the rail and stare down her fierce blue nemesis.

Carrie silently cursed Analee once again. Her employer had ordered Carrie to be responsible for delivering her jewels and clothes, since she and her *amour du jour* had been delayed in Rome.

Probably due to an orgy at the Coliseum.

The yacht dipped sideways, righted itself, then

lurched to the opposite angle. Analee snatched at the slippery, globe-shaped jewelry case, hugging it to her body and wishing she could be anywhere but here.

"You're turning positively green, dear."

Analee took several panting breaths, then met the gaze of the elderly woman, who had taken the leather-tufted seat opposite. The flower poised on her head was still trying to make its escape, but due to the effect the flapping had had on her stomach, Carrie averted her eyes.

The woman smiled at her and dug into her voluminous crocheted bag, withdrawing a tissue.

"I'm Greta Peery."

"Pleased to meet you," Carrie said through clenched teeth, gratefully accepting the gift and dabbing at the clammy film of perspiration dotting her face.

"Didn't you take any medicine before you came?" Greta inquired, closing her bag, then slipping a hundred dollar bill between the pages of the hardback novel she'd been reading.

A hundred dollars for a bookmark? You've really stumbled into the Long Island "horsey" set.

"I couldn't take…anything," Carrie said, tipping her head back so that the cool air drifted over her brow. "Makes me drowsy."

And if anything happened to one piece of Analee's luggage—or, heaven forbid, her jewelry case—Carrie's head would be mounted on the wall in the woman's hobby room, next to the African water buffalo.

The older woman made a *tsking* sound with her tongue. "Poor thing. Me, I get a little queasy now and again, but as long as I bring something to get my mind off my tummy, I'm content as a clam."

Hitching closer, the woman held up the book she'd been reading, exposing a dramatic black-and-gold cover. The author's name snagged Carrie's attention as completely as if it had been formed from flashing neon, endlessly repeating its message.

Analee Adler, Analee Adler, Analee Adler...

Carrie grimaced. Even now, with her employer halfway across the globe, Carrie couldn't escape Analee's influence—or a potent reminder of the piles of work awaiting Carrie as soon as she returned to Manhattan.

"Have you read any of the Princess Anushka books?" Greta inquired, her features becoming flushed with excitement. "Of course you have," she supplied before Carrie could reply. "Everyone has read them—men, as well as women. I hear Hollywood is already planning several movies based on the characters. If it were my choice, I think Anushka should be played by..."

The words washed over Carrie in a wave. She continued to stare at the book jacket, at the author's name, at the title, *Mistress of Moscow.* Not for the first time, Carrie felt a twinge of—

Of what? Jealousy? Anger? Pride? Ownership?

Carrie's eyes darted to Greta's lips, watching

them move, but not really absorbing the sounds that emerged. What would this elderly lady say if Carrie admitted to having written that book? That particular book, as well as thirteen of the other fourteen Princess Anushka novels?

She wouldn't believe you.

Naturally she wouldn't believe her. Why should she? A person would have to be crazy to proclaim herself the author of the bestsellers without proof to back up such a comment. Especially since Carrie's claim to such fame was limited. Originally, Carrie had come to Analee as a personal secretary. But when Analee suffered a case of shingles soon before the deadline of her second novel, Carrie had "helped" her employer by finishing and polishing the book.

Finishing and polishing? her inner voice snorted. *You wrote all but the first five pages!*

And by doing so, she had become Analee's "secret." Under the guise of being Analee's assistant, Carrie wrote all of the novels now—from start to finish—for a portion of the royalties. Analee, on the other hand, accepted *all* the glory and fame.

Pushing her gloom aside, Carrie forced herself to concentrate on what Greta was saying.

"Of course, the first book in the series was horrrrible." She pursed her lips, as if the memory left a bad taste in her mouth. "But I forgave Ms. Adler for her inexperience. Since then, she hasn't disappointed me a bit. I simply *adorrre* Princess Anushka and her personal bodyguard, Boris." The woman shivered in delight. ''Too bad he was injured in the war,'' she murmured, as if she were speaking of a real man and not a fictional character. ''He's so handsome, so intense, sooo...'' The elderly woman growled like a tiger. ''It's so tragic that he can't...that he can never...that in bed he isn't able to...you know...'' she finished in a whisper.

Carrie *did* know. She knew all too well. Damn it, it was *she* who had invented Boris, *she* who had written all of the World War I espionage thrillers.

Even if she could never claim the fact publicly.

''Are you familiar with this novel, dear?''

Intimately.

''Mmm...'' Carrie said noncommittally, her stomach pitching as the launch plunged through a large swell.

The woman continued as if Carrie hadn't spoken. ''It's all about the seedy underworld in Moscow. It begins when the Russian troops are summoned to return home from the trenches of France to help control the civil unrest in their own country. Anushka and Boris are playing a deadly game of cat and mouse, pretending to be lovers in order to allay suspicion. They—''

The blast of the yacht's horn interrupted the monologue and, bending sideways, Carrie was relieved to see that the vessel was mere yards from the pier. Another, much smaller boat had maneuvered into position next to the floating docks, and a man dressed in scuba gear and a wet suit was slinging his oxygen tanks over one shoulder.

Unconsciously, Carrie half stood, wanting to catch her first glimpse of the famous—or *infamous*—Babcock estates. Not for the first time, she envied Analee's assumption of an invitation to a fortnight of period costumes, elaborate whodunit games, daytime picnics and sporting activities. But most of all, she envied Analee for having the opportunity to meet the elusive Edward Remington Babcock—*the* most eligible bachelor. He was reputed to be the fourth-richest man in the world, an athlete, an avid human-rights spokesman and lord and master of the immense Babcock dynasty—a conglomeration of industry, financing, and literary pursuits. He even owned the parent company of Analee Adler's publishing house.

His monetary accomplishments aside, there was so much more to the man that was intriguing. His personal life lay hidden in mystery. No one knew much of anything about him at all—and gossip was rife as to his appearance and daily routines. As an infant, he'd survived a terrible kidnapping ordeal. Since then, there'd been no published photographs of him. Indeed, it was rumored that he clung to his anonymity so that he could mingle with his employees as a common worker and thereby analyze the true success of his projects.

Carrie bit her lip, straining to see beyond the waves dashing against the rocky coastline. According to the invitation, Edward Babcock would be at the party—in disguise, no doubt—ready to see to the comfort of his guests.

If Carrie had been invited, she was sure she could have unearthed his true identity. She would consider it her own personal challenge—much like Princess Anushka unearthing a spy. After all, Carrie had proved over and over again that she had a talent for covert investigation techniques. Hadn't she kept her own role as Anushka's creator secret for years?

Now fully standing, Carrie leaned over the rail, squinting against the dazzling light glinting off the cool, deep water. Eagerly she scanned the stark bluff and the steep staircase carved into the rocks. But from this angle, there was no sign of the house itself, no sign of any habitation at all, save for the frogman alighting from the motorboat.

If only Carrie could stay on this island. If only she could claim her identity as Babcock Publishing's most lucrative fiction author. If only she could be a part of such an extravagant affair. Just once. How she would love to inundate herself in the fantasy, to become something other than a mousy secretary. If only...

The horn blasted again, and Carrie started, automatically reaching for the railing. But the dashing waves had made the brass wet, and her fingers slipped. Crying out, she flailed her arms in an attempt to steady herself.

Instantly she realized her mistake. The slippery gold-inlaid jewelry case flew from her grip and arced through the air. As if in slow motion, Carrie saw the ball-shaped container spinning away, then falling, falling, until it dropped into the ocean with a huge, heavy splash.

"No. Please!" Carrie cried out, one foot already on the railing. "Somebody help me. Please!"

An image of Analee Adler screaming about the loss of her jewels flashed through her brain, and Carrie panicked even more. "Help me! Somebody help me!"

Then, before Carrie could determine how best to save the case herself, the launch bumped against the pier and she lost her precarious balance. Much to her horror, she felt her body being thrown into the air. Then she was falling, falling, smacking against the hard surface of the water and sinking down, down, down, into the cold, merciless depths....

EDWARD BABCOCK heard the scream as he was securing his speedboat to the pier. He whirled just in time to catch a glimpse of a dark-haired woman teetering near the railing of the vessel. Then she crashed into the churning waves.

Grimacing, Edward waited, expecting an angry guest to surface and demand to be taken to the island's owner, but within seconds he realized that the woman was in trouble. She tried valiantly to surface—one slight, delicate hand flailing in an attempt to swim—then she disappeared completely, and the water became still.

"Woman overboard!" an elderly lady screamed from the launch. "Woman overboard!"

Swearing, Edward dropped his tanks and dived

into the ocean. His eyes stinging against the on-slaught of salt and sediment, he tried to locate a shape, a flash of color—anything to help him to find the damsel in distress.

Just as his lungs began to burn, he glanced to his left and saw her, drifting beneath the bottom of the launch, her head bumping against the hull as the current began tugging her away from Babcock Island.

Kicking with all his might, Edward caught up with the slight figure and snagged her around the waist. Horrified, he realized that she wasn't fighting him. Instead, her body was as limp as a rag doll's. A bad sign. A bad sign, indeed.

Summoning the last of his strength, Edward fought to reach the sunlight gleaming over his head. As he broke the surface, he took a deep gulp of air, then moved toward the pier. When he was halfway there, two crew members from the launch jumped into the sea beside him, taking the weight of the stranger, then lifting her toward the captain, who stood on the planks.

"Is she breathing?" Edward asked as he lapped his forearms over the end of the dock and tried to fill his own aching chest with oxygen.

"No," the older man said as he swept a finger inside her mouth to check for obstructions. "I think she swallowed a lot of water."

By the time Edward had pulled himself onto the dock, Captain Hobbs had tipped her head and pinched her nose, but for some inexplicable reason,

Edward felt driven to resuscitate the woman himself, to ensure that she was safe, that she lived.

"I'll do that," Edward said gruffly, taking Hobbs's place. He knew Captain Hobbs had a heart condition, so he wasn't surprised when the man eagerly backed away, issuing instructions to his men.

"Go get help!" he shouted to one of the security guards who had appeared at the top of the bluff. Then Hobbs pointed to the crew members pulling themselves up the launch ladder. "You two take the guests to the house and inform Dickerson of what's happened."

"Yes, sir!"

The men quickly complied, escorting the half-dozen reluctant passengers from the launch as Edward laid his lips over the stranger's and began to fill her lungs with air. To his immense relief, after three puffs, the woman jerked beneath him.

Lifting his head, he watched her lashes flutter, the tips of her fingers twitch. Then she violently twisted to the side and began retching into the ocean.

"That's right, that's right," Edward crooned, his heart tightening oddly in his chest. Edging closer, he wrapped an arm around her waist and helped her to half sit, half collapse, against him as she coughed. Not sure what else he should do, Edward cradled her slight frame against his body, smoothing her dark, tangled hair away from her cheeks.

As he did so, he was struck by the purity of her features—slender brows, eyes framed with thick, dark lashes, an aquiline nose and a full, rosebud-shaped mouth. She really was quite beautiful. One of those fragile creatures who, in the nineteenth century, would have been considered a "porcelain princess."

But this was no piece of china. No, her body was strangely vital, even after her close brush with death. She smelled of seawater and some exotic perfume, and her skin...

It was the kind of skin that begged a man to touch it.

Again, his heart made an odd sort of twisting sensation in his chest, and he took a deep breath. His nerves weren't nearly as steady as usual—and for a man accustomed to handling a variety of crises each day, the fact was unsettling.

His brow creased. Who could this woman possibly be? Long before Edward finalized his guest list, his security men had investigated each possible candidate, providing Edward with photographs and biographical data. Edward had never seen *this* face in any of the dossiers given to him. If he had, he would have remembered her instantly.

But if she wasn't a guest, then what was she doing on his island? If she hadn't been issued a personal invitation, she would have to leave. That was one rule Edward insisted upon. His parties would not be compromised by gate-crashers.

At long last, the woman's breathing eased and her lashes puddled against her cheeks. To his relief, he noted a tinge of pink flooding her pale skin.

"I—" The word was barely a croak, and she

lifted a hand to her throat. A fragile hand. A grace-
ful hand.

Edward reached around her slight body and
placed a finger over her mouth, absorbing the
warmth that had been absent from her lips mere
moments before. As he did so, her eyes opened, and
he found himself staring into irises the color of
black olives.

For several seconds, he was trapped in her gaze,
in her confusion and unease. Then he managed to
muster enough of his faculties to say, "Don't try to
talk yet. You've had a shock. Get your wind back
first."

She nodded and probed the top of her head with
her fingertips. A grimace wrinkled her nose, and
Edward fought the urge to chuckle in delight at her
expression.

"You also whacked your head against the side of
the boat," he explained.

She looked up at him, her eyes wide, the color
of her pupils barely distinguishable from the faceted
depths of her irises. He'd never seen eyes that color
before—so rich, so intriguing.

"What…happened?" the woman finally managed to croak.

"You fell from the launch." When she didn't
respond, he added, "The one bringing you to Babcock Island."

The stranger's expression remained as blank as a
motionless pool. "Who…"

"Who am I?" Edward was used to dodging such

questions, but for the first time in years, he found himself tempted to tell her the truth.

Go ahead and tell her.

Tell her? And have her metamorphose into some sort of sycophant or, worse yet, treat him with the distant respect one might offer alien royalty?

"I'm just an innocent bystander," he supplied instead, wishing that the trappings of his family fortune didn't require such subterfuge.

"You...look like...a frog...."

She began coughing again, and Edward pushed the neoprene hood of his wet suit off his face and raked his fingers through his hair.

"Better?" he inquired when the woman grew still again, her eyes studying him with the same intensity an art student might give the *Mona Lisa.*

"Mmm..." Her lashes were heavy now, her eyes barely open at all. "You look just like..."

Edward's heart lurched. "Like who?" he demanded.

After years of anonymity, had his true identity finally been found out?

Chapter Two

Edward's heart thudded in his ears.

"Who?" he demanded again, more loudly this time. "Who do I look like?"

Damn it, was this woman a reporter who had infiltrated his security system? Was she some tabloid photographer intent on exposing his face to the world?

He shook her slightly, and a half smile tugged at the corner of her lips.

"You...look just like..."

Edward bent closer to catch the whisper.

"...just like...Borrrrr..."

He looked like Bor? Bor who?

Or had she meant he looked like a *bore?*

A snicker of relief burst from his lips, but then he froze. Damn it, he wasn't a bore. He wasn't at all like a good portion of his guests—suffering from ennui and intent on amusing themselves at great expense.

Who *was* this woman?

Since the stranger in his arms was clearly exhausted from her ordeal, Edward slid one arm beneath her knees and the other around her shoulders. He'd have to carry her to the top of the bluff. Heaven only knew he couldn't afford to have her tumble down the rocky staircase. Such an accident would be both emotionally and financially damaging. After all, who wouldn't sue Edward Remington Babcock for such carelessness? As it was, he'd have to instruct his lawyers to look into this woman's fall from the boat. Edward wasn't sure if he could be held liable for her plight.

The woman moaned slightly as he shifted her.

Drawing his mind away from business, law and the family fortune, Edward stated, "There's a doctor in the security bungalow. Hold tight and I'll carry you up to the top."

The stranger didn't answer. Edward wondered briefly if she'd swooned, sinking back into a worrisome unconsciousness. Even if she had, such a reaction was to be expected, wasn't it? She couldn't possibly be seriously injured.

Could she?

Scooping her against his body, he marveled at the slight weight of her body and the iciness still clinging to her wet clothing. He'd taken only a few steps when she shifted anxiously.

"No. M-my… The bags…"

"They'll be brought up to the house. Don't worry."

"But…"

"Shh, now."

Edward wasn't sure whether or not she heard him. Her head suddenly lolled backward and she drooped against his chest. If not for the faint rattling of her respiration, he would have thought her lungs had failed her.

"Sir!"

The call came from the top of the bluff, and Edward immediately recognized Dr. Little's voice. Squinting against the late sun, he noted Captain Hobbs, Doc Little and three security men nearing the limestone steps.

"Don't bother to come down," Edward called. "I'll bring her up to you."

The moment Edward reached the summit, one of the guards tried to take the woman from his arms. Following instincts he couldn't quite fathom, Edward shook his head. Oddly, he couldn't bear to think of someone else holding her so intimately. Instead, he proceeded toward the small bungalow that housed the infirmary.

The rest of the entourage followed wordlessly, already efficiently evaluating the situation. Doc Little rushed into the wing containing the clinic, holding the door open for the group.

"Over here, please," he said, gesturing to an examining table.

Edward gently placed the woman on the padded surface, then signaled for the guards to retreat from the room and close the door. Through the frosted glass he could see their looming shapes denying access to anyone who might prove curious enough to interrupt the proceedings.

"I hear we had an accident at the pier," Doc said as he snapped rubber gloves over his pudgy fingers. He reached for his stethoscope.

"She fell from the launch," Edward said succinctly, planting his hands on the counter behind him and resting his hips against the edge. His posture remained loose and unassuming, but he couldn't keep his fingers from curling around the lip of the shiny tile behind him.

"What did you do, Captain Hobbs? Hit a speed bump?" Doc teased.

"Very funny," Hobbs growled, far from amused. Clearly, the man was shaken by the entire episode.

Doc chuckled, his corpulent belly jiggling like a bowl of gelatin. "Touchy, touchy, touchy. Surely you can take a joke." His eyes twinkled for one more moment, and then his features became serious and intent. "Let's see how she is," he murmured, reaching for the woman's wrist and timing her pulse by the oversize clock hanging above the door.

"Her heartbeat is strong enough," he commented, releasing her arm and positioning the stethoscope in his ears. "You revived her, Edward?"

Edward shifted his weight to one leg and crossed his feet at the ankles in a show of nonchalance. "Yes, but I only gave her two or three puffs of air before she started breathing on her own."

"Mmm." The doctor checked the woman's pupils and made a cursory inspection of her skull with his fingertips. "I was told she might have hit her head."

"I saw her bump it against the boat once, but there's no telling if she hit it again before I found her."

"Mmm-hmm," Doc mumbled, concentrating on his patient. "There is a goose egg appearing on the back of her skull, but I don't feel any other apparent signs of swelling." He winked in Captain Hobbs's direction. "Maybe you got lucky."

Hobbs scowled, but before he could comment on the doctor's words, the stranger stirred.

Edward took a breath, holding it in anticipation, as did the others. They all watched intently as the woman's fingers curled into her palms, then relaxed and began to search the surface she lay upon.

"That's a good girl," Doc Little crooned. "Time to rise and shine and tell us how you're feeling. Don't be alarmed, you just fainted, probably due to the shock of the accident. You'll be right as rain soon enough."

A soft groan eased from the stranger's lips, and the doctor beamed and straightened. "That's a good girl. Open your eyes, sweetie."

Doc Little continued to watch her intently, all the while removing his stethoscope and looping it around his neck. Then, when the woman's lashes fluttered faintly, he folded his hands at the approximate location of his navel and peered at the woman with the utmost concentration.

"I see no evident injury other than the knot on her head," he offered under his breath. "Her lungs are clear, although my guess is the salt water has probably burned the back of her throat. Her voice will be rather husky for a few days, and..."

He lapsed into silence, as if his speech had fallen behind in its struggle to keep up with the whirring of his brain.

"Should we fly her to the mainland?" Edward said after several long, agonizing moments.

The doctor started. "No. I don't see any call for such drastic measures. But I wouldn't be surprised if she has a mild concussion, perhaps even some short-term memory loss and confusion for a day or two. I want her watched for the evening. Someone will have to wake her every few hours, ask her questions like 'What's your name?' and 'What day is it?' By morning, if we see any other signs of trauma, I'll arrange to have her flown to the nearest hospital."

"So somebody has to stay with her all night long?" Hobbs asked.

"I'll make the necessary arrangements right away," a voice said, coming from the direction of the doorway.

Edward grinned when Doc jumped. Clutching a hand to his chest, the physician turned to confront the regal gentleman who had entered the clinic without so much as a creak of the floorboards.

"Jeez, Dickerson. Don't do that!"

"Don't do what, sir?" the man asked, although

it was clear that he was accustomed to surprising the man and had grown to relish such occasions.

Edward quickly disguised his grin by rubbing his hand over his mouth. Dickerson, the butler who oversaw the house, had been torturing Doc Little for years with his ability to slip into a room unnoticed.

"Would you prefer I wore bells, Mr. Little?"

"*Dr.* Little to you, you limey good-for-nothing—"

Knowing that he should interrupt the argument now, Edward inserted, "Dickerson, arrange to have Miss...Whoever-She-Is transferred to my mother's suites in the east wing."

Hobbs's jaw dropped.

Little choked.

Dickerson managed to maintain his bland facade, but his brows rose infinitesimally.

"The *east* wing, sir?"

"Yes. This woman is my responsibility until we can determine who she is and why she's attempting to crash the gala. I'd like to keep her separated from the other guests as much as possible in the interim."

The object of their discussion moaned softly, her hand gripping the edge of the table beneath her.

Dickerson clearly disapproved of the plan. "But, sir, I can arrange to have Maggie or—"

Edward interrupted smoothly. "The staff has enough to do, with the party in full swing. I'll stay with the woman tonight."

Edward wasn't exactly sure why he felt it nec-

essary that *he* be the one to care for the stranger—
let alone why he was determined to have her en-
sconced in the most private wing of Babcock
Mansion. He only knew that if someone was going
to watch her sleep, stay with her through the night,
ask her questions, it had to be him.

Wrenching away from the possible sources of his
inexplicable possessiveness for the woman, Edward
straightened and assumed the mask of command he
was accustomed to wearing.

"I'm going to my own rooms to shower and
change. I will expect to meet you, Dickerson, and
our guest in Mother's room twenty minutes from
now. Have two of the guards put her on a stretcher
and bring her up through the tunnels so none of the
other guests see her."

"Yes, sir."

The butler was solicitous—even diffident. But
Edward wasn't fooled. Dickerson clearly disapproved of the outlined plan. He was just too polite
and well trained to say anything more.

Eager to avoid further questions from his staff,
Edward pushed himself away from the counter and
strode to the door. As he opened it, he was arrested
by the rustle of clothing when the woman stirred
again. Pausing, he glanced back at her, holding her
gaze for one long, aching moment.

Her eyes flickered as she adjusted to the overhead
lights. Twisting her head, she met Edward's gaze
with complete lucidity. In their dark brown depths,
Edward read the woman's confusion, pique and

pain. Then, sighing, she whispered, "You...bor..." and collapsed again.

Grimacing, Edward made his way from the infirmary to the rear staircase located at the end of the hall. From there, he took one of the tunnels that led to the mansion and branched off into various secret passageways. The tunnels were a relic of the Roaring Twenties, when bootlegging had been in its prime. One of Edward's great-uncles—a black sheep of the family—had not felt in the least uneasy about augmenting his own wealth through crime.

Edward grinned to himself. Unfortunately, the man had lost his ill-gotten gains in the stock-market crash, then spent ten years in a penitentiary. No one could have accused *that* man of being a bore.

Frowning, Edward ran his fingers through his still-wet hair. Maybe he should get a haircut or something.

TODAY was going to be a wonderful day. A *marvelous* day.

For one tiny, indulgent moment, she snuggled deeper into the satin sheets and hugged the pillow to her cheek. She'd had such odd dreams all night long. Dreams of a man leaning over her bed, caressing her with his eyes, whispering sweet nothings into her ears.

Had it only been a dream?

Yawning, she regretfully pushed the quilted coverlet away and stretched her hands over her head. A sharp pain shot through her skull, and she winced.

How in the world had she managed to acquire such a rotten headache? She couldn't remember drinking anything at all, but if she didn't know any better, she would have sworn she had a doozy of a hangover.

Rolling into the softness of the pillow, she grimaced again when the pain doubled, centering from a spot at the back of her skull.

What in the world?

Lifting one well-manicured hand, she examined her scalp with her fingers. The instant she located a lump the size of a golf ball on the back of her head, she frowned, then peered at the unfamiliar masculine print of the oversize pajama top she wore. Funny, she didn't remember arriving on the island, let alone undressing herself...

Of course! She'd been on her way to Babcock Island in the launch when that incompetent captain threw her into the water and ruined her new gown. Blast the man, anyway! She'd had the dress for less than a week, and yesterday had been her first opportunity to wear it. If the captain had offered some sort of warning...

With a cluck of her tongue, she muttered, "Spilt milk," to herself, arched her back and yawned again. She'd simply have to see that the man was severely reprimanded for his carelessness. After all, she, Princess Anushka, demanded the very best from her employees. She should be able to expect the same from that Babcock fellow's men, as well.

Throwing the covers aside, she swung her feet to

the floor, then smiled in delight at the sturdy masculine frame stretched out on the floor.

At least Boris had never failed her. Dear, dear Boris—her friend, her companion, her bodyguard. If not for the injury he had sustained in the war...

She sighed heavily. More spilt milk. What was done was done. *Que sera, sera.* One couldn't change fate. Not even Princess Anushka had that power.

Studying the pajama top she wore, then the matching fabric of the bottoms Boris had donned, she realized that he must have brought her to this room, undressed her, then supplied her with the unusual sleepwear. Generally she wouldn't allow anything but silk for her lingerie.

Smiling coyly, Anushka used her toe to nudge the figure lying facedown on the carpet. Despite the man's...accident, she couldn't help delighting in the firm masculine flesh exposed above the sheet he'd taken from her bed.

Poor Boris. When would he learn to gather his own linens instead of dismantling hers? How he ever managed to sleep so deeply while stretched out on a hard floor, yet still have the ability to rise at the first hint of danger, she would never know. If he would only allow the maids to bring him an extra pillow or two, she was sure, he wouldn't be nearly so grouchy in the morning.

"Wake up," she said cheerily, poking him again, her eyes sweeping over his dark, curling hair, his muscular shoulders, the crease of his spine. So handsome, so supposedly virile.

Life could be cruel at times.

Rising, she stepped over his prone shape, striding to the mountains of leather suitcases, hatboxes and trunks left in the corner of her room. Opening one, she discovered to her delight that the containers had already been emptied. Throwing open one of the doors to a nearby armoire, she noted that her things had been unpacked, pressed and stored to her satisfaction.

She bobbed her head in approval. Thus far, her accommodations at Babcock Mansion had proved to be adequate. Evidently, she'd been completely shaken by her accident. She didn't quite remember being taken to her room and retiring for the night. But the household help had been dedicated enough to take care of her things and see that Boris was settled.

Glancing at the bed, at the remains of a meal tray on the bedside table, then at the man on the floor, she folded her arms under her breasts. Yes. Babcock Mansion *was* proving to be a pleasant surprise.

Immediately her thoughts sobered as she remembered her purpose in being here. Babcock Mansion might appear to be a dream come true, but, by now, she was sure that the estate was rife with danger. Only last week Anushka had discovered that the mansion had become the hideout for a notorious band of cat burglars known only by their code name, MEOW. If Anushka hadn't intercepted one of the group's messages on the wireless hidden in her bookcase behind a volume of very poor American poetry, the jewelry thieves would probably have had free rein at Babcock's soiree and stolen the guests blind. Even now, they were most likely plotting and scheming their nefarious plans.

Which was the very reason she and Boris should hurry downstairs and begin their investigation.

Marching to the bed, Anushka poked her bodyguard with her foot again. This time in the leg. A firm leg. An athlete's leg.

No, not an athlete. A soldier. Anushka had plucked Boris from the trenches of France and nursed him back to the picture of health. He was fully cured.

Well, he was *nearly* cured, she amended silently. Nothing could remedy the injury which had robbed him of his ability to…

You know.

"Get up, Boris. We have to go downstairs and begin mingling with the guests. We have suspects to gather, after all."

Boris shifted. Without moving from his stomach, he propped himself on his elbows and pressed the palms of his hands to his eyes. Then he rolled to his back and stared up at Anushka.

His eyes were so clear, so blue, so brilliant. They had only to settle upon a woman to make her infinitely aware of her femininity. Not even the time Anushka and Boris had spent together had weakened the power of his regard.

"You're awake," he commented, his voice gruff with sleep.

"Of course I'm awake." She pointed to the ornate golden clock on her nightstand. "It's nearly noon."

He blinked, rubbed his eyes again, then curled to a sitting position, the muscles of his chest and abdomen rippling, the sheet dropping to expose his navel.

"You are a god in your own right," she murmured lowly, her gaze riveted to the array of flesh and musculature exposed. Although the compliment would probably cause Boris to grow conceited, she could not have held her tongue. Not when the man's sheer masculinity thrummed in the air like a hidden current of electricity.

Boris peered at her carefully, then frowned and said, "You aren't so bad yourself."

The words were enough to cause a delicious warmth to gather deep in her stomach, but she resolutely ignored the sensation. Time was of the essence. She couldn't wallow in fantasies of what might have been.

What an awful war.

What a cruel, hurtful war.

Might the Huns be damned for all eternity for what they had done to Boris.

Turning on her toe, she strode to the wardrobe, putting a buffer between her and the man who attended to her safety. Whipping open armoire doors and elaborate drawers, she familiarized herself with

the placement of her things. Then, returning to one
of the top shelves, she chose a pair of black silk tap
pants, as well as a matching garter, sheer hosiery
and an embroidered brassiere.

"I intend to bathe now. See to it that my breakfast is brought up immediately."

Then, knowing Boris would take care of such
mundane matters as food, she disappeared into the
bathroom and shut the door firmly behind her.

EDWARD sat for several minutes, feeling as if he'd
missed something during the first coherent conversation he had with his near-drowning victim. Try as
he might, he couldn't make much sense out of the
exchange that had just occurred. The woman had
been polite, for the most part, lucid, capable, and
yet...

He was *definitely* missing something. Such as
"Hello, my name is..." or "Who are you?" or
"Thanks for rescuing me." Maybe "Thanks for
loaning me your pajama tops while my clothes were
cleaned."

Shaking his head, Edward stood, then hitched up
the waistband of the corresponding pajama bottoms.
Whoever his uninvited guest might be, she was bold
as brass and twice as blunt.

Without warning, he was reminded of the heart-
felt tribute the woman had given him. Had he really
heard her correctly? Had this stranger actually murmured, *"You are a god in your own right"*?

No. He must have been mistaken. No woman would utter such a thing to a stranger.

But she'd said it to him. He was sure he'd caught the correct words.

His lips twitched in a smile that was both embarrassed and pleased. "A god, huh?" he said to himself in disbelief.

Automatically he reached for the receiver of the bedside phone. Before he could pick it up, however, a muted tap came from the direction of the white-and-gilt double doors. Sighing, Edward realized that Dickerson had once again sensed the need for his services long before they were actually requested.

Stretching muscles that ached from a night spent sleeping on the floor, Edward made his way to the heavy door. Twisting the knob, he peered around the edge, blearily acknowledging Dickerson's tall, gaunt frame and the covered tray he held. Motioning to the man to proceed with his duties, Edward moved into the small sitting area adjoining the bedroom and collapsed onto a brocade-covered settee.

Without making a sound, Dickerson followed him, set the tray on a small table, then poured coffee from a carafe into a delicate china cup and extended it to his employer.

Edward gladly took the brew, hoping the jolt of caffeine would help him gather his wits and make some sort of sense out of this whole situation.

After several moments, Dickerson delicately inquired, "The lady is..."

"Bathing," Edward intoned, with more emotion

than was necessary for such a simple response. Taking another sip of the strong coffee, he tried to pierce the haze of his exhaustion, wondering if the woman had somehow introduced herself while he was struggling to awaken.

No. He was sure she hadn't. He vaguely remembered being poked in the leg. Then someone had accused him of being a bore again. Other than that, he couldn't remember a single important detail until the moment he'd opened his eyes and seen her towering over his prone form, a good deal of leg exposed to him.

"Tell me, Dickerson," Edward asked suddenly, "do I look boring to you?"

"No, sir."

Edward was gratified by the quick response.

"Then why does she keep calling me a bore?"

"She calls you a bore, sir?" One of Dickerson's brows arched.

Edward shifted uncomfortably. "As far as I can make out the word."

Although his expression didn't change, Edward sensed that Dickerson was highly amused by this information.

"Do I look like a bore, Dickerson?"

"I wouldn't know, sir."

"No. Of course you wouldn't," Edward agreed absently, knowing that Dickerson would never admit to entertaining any negative impressions of his employer.

"Perhaps, as you said, you misunderstood her comment," Dickerson offered.

"You could be right. After all, we still don't know who that blasted woman is, let alone how she thinks. For all I know, she could be offering me some sort of tribute."

Dickerson's lips twitched in an obvious struggle not to reply to such an enticing comment. "You could be right," he finally said. After a slight pause, he asked, "Will there be anything else, sir?"

Edward shook his head. His temples throbbed from the quick movement. He'd had little or no sleep all night long. He'd been so sure that his patient would expire if he didn't watch her every single moment. Now his body was protesting his obvious disregard for his own needs.

"Go on downstairs and tend to the other guests, Dickerson."

"As you wish."

The balding, droopy-jowled man backed to the door. He looked so like a morose basset hound that Edward had to avert his eyes to hide his involuntary amusement.

The man was about to slip into the hall when Edward inquired, "Is it my hair? Do you think it's too conservative?"

But if Dickerson had an opinion on the matter, he chose to keep it to himself. Pulling the door closed behind him, he silently disappeared from sight.

"Damn," Edward muttered, raking his fingers

through his hair. Maybe he *should* arrange for a new cut.

Sighing, Edward drained his coffee. He was refilling his cup when he heard the creak of the bathroom door.

"Darling, I need your help."

The porcelain nearly fell from Edward's fingers. He blinked, then blinked again, but the vision hadn't changed.

His guest was still standing in front of him...dressed in nothing but the black silk undergarments she'd chosen minutes ago.

Chapter Three

The woman didn't seem the least bit embarrassed or self-conscious. On the contrary. She stepped to within inches of his body, then turned, presenting her back.

"Would you be a dear and hook me?"

The ends of her brassiere dangled below her shoulder blades, making him intimately aware of her smooth, ivory skin.

"Well?" she demanded, peering coyly over her shoulder. "My arms are curiously stiff, so I would appreciate your efforts."

His mouth grew so dry, Edward could barely smile. But then, he wasn't about to refuse. It had been a very long time since he had had the pleasure of helping a woman with her morning toilet.

Her skin was warm against his knuckles. Soft. Like rose petals. An exotic fragrance rose from her body and hair, infusing his senses and causing him to fumble before connecting the hooks.

"*Merci beaucoup*," the woman offered breezily as she turned on her toes. Without a care, she padded to the wardrobe, removed a pair of period pumps, and slipped her feet into them.

"I must be losing weight," she commented. "My shoes have been fitting a bit large lately."

Edward scrambled to find something to say, but she continued as if she hadn't expected a reply. "Thank heavens loose-fitting clothes are all the rage. I wouldn't dream of participating in this gala if my gowns weren't right."

Still frozen in place, Edward watched the woman's every move. Reaching inside the wardrobe, she withdrew a drop-waisted suit of rust-colored satin and crepe. Even from his spot in the sitting room, Edward could tell that the garment was a genuine antique. Rhinestones glittered from the mock belt at the hips and at the hem of the knee-length jacket.

Enthralled, Edward absently lowered his coffee cup as the woman lifted the dress over her head, then wriggled and twitched until the fabric shimmied into place, coating her figure like liquid ink. Then, after running a comb through her blunt bob, she lifted on tiptoe and removed a straw cloche from one of the upper shelves.

As she dragged the close-fitting hat over her head so that it framed her face and emphasized her dark eyes, she sauntered toward Edward, her hips moving from side to side, the rhinestones glittering, her black hose limning the sweet shape of her slender ankles.

"Good, you remembered," she commented as she sank into one of the chairs and crossed her legs with a whisper of silk rubbing silk. Reaching for a plate, she chose three strawberries, spread a napkin over her lap and began to nibble on the fruit.

"Re—" Edward cleared his throat and tried again. "Remembered? What did I remember?"

"That I have devoted myself to eating fruit at every meal in order to underscore my loyalty to the labor movement."

"Labor movement?" he echoed blankly.

"Now, Boris. We've been over this before. You know I feel driven to see the plight of the peasants improved."

Peasants?

Boris? Who was Boris?

A slow chill crept through his veins. Doc Little had warned him that the woman might suffer some slight memory loss and confusion—but did that include mistaking Edward for somebody else?

"Since I cannot voice myself too publicly without endangering my intelligence-gathering, I've promised to eat more fruit and vegetables in a silent show of solidarity for my fellow countrymen."

Intelligence-gathering? Silent show of solidarity?

Edward carefully set his cup on the tray and intently studied the woman. But the sight of this stranger, clad in little more than a few layers of silk and satin, regarding him with those dark, olive-colored eyes, made concentration difficult.

His body began to respond accordingly, and he abruptly stood.

"I have to get dressed."

"You do that. And see that you wear something devastatingly handsome. We're supposed to be lovers, you know."

That statement hit him like a punch to his gut.

"We're *what?*"

She waved a dismissing hand. "We've gone over this already. I know you don't approve, but desperate times demand desperate measures."

Edward blinked, wondering if the *real* Boris would soon be pounding down the door and demanding a reckoning.

"Who *are* you?" he asked slowly, hoping that the blunt question wouldn't further muddle her thinking.

She laughed in delight. "Oh, Boris. You're such a tease. You know very well that we can't afford to assume false identities for this particular case. For the next few weeks, we will play our parts as close to the real truth as possible. To all those we encounter, we are who we are. Princess Anushka and her devoted bodyguard, Boris. Only this time, we must make everyone believe that we are madly, passionately, in love. That way, when you publicly propose and offer me the ring, the bait will have been carefully set and the trap well sprung."

"Princess Anushka?" Edward repeated in disbelief. Now he knew he was in trouble. This woman had not only suffered a head injury, but she'd somehow confused her own identity with that of a character from one of Babcock Publishing's most successful series of novels.

She had to be afflicted with something more than short-term memory loss. Good hell, what if she'd suffered some sort of irreversible brain damage?

Panic surged through his body. The woman claiming to be Princess Anushka seemed suddenly that much smaller and fragile to him.

Edward speared the air with his index finger. "Don't move," he ordered, knowing he had to find Doc Little. Immediately. "I'll be right back."

As he strode through the double doors, his visitor called, "Don't forget to dress properly for our ruse, Boris. No uniforms this time. Understand?"

Glancing at her one last time, he weakly said, "Sure. Whatever you say."

BY THE TIME Edward had returned to his room, he was slightly calmer. But only slightly.

Seeing that Dickerson had laid out his costume for the day, Edward dressed in a pair of wool trousers, a crisp white shirt, and a 1920s-vintage vest— but only to save time. Throughout his toilet, he was consumed with worry.

What would make a woman confuse herself with a character from one of Analee Adler's books? Had she been reading one of the novels on the launch? Was she an avid fan? A disgusted critic?

As soon as the last cuff link was in place, he strode to the door, paused, then returned to the bathroom. Since no one but his employees knew that he was really the host of this event, he couldn't afford to look out of character. He would have to see that he gave every appearance of being a guest, intent on fun and games.

Even if fun and games were the last things on his mind.

Quickly he rubbed pomade on his hair, then combed the unruly strands into a severe, conservative style reminiscent of F. Scott Fitzgerald and Gatsby. As he did so, his mind kept dwelling on the same thoughts over and over, like a record needle stuck in a groove.

What was wrong with his guest? And how should he handle the situation?

With kid gloves, most likely. He couldn't afford to startle her and make her condition worse.

Throwing the brush on the dressing table, he shrugged into his suit coat and tugged at his starched cuffs. This whole situation was partly his own fault, he supposed. He should have watched her more closely throughout the night. Twice he'd gone to the security bungalow to check on the list of guests who had arrived.

What a stupid mistake. He shouldn't have been so worried about gate-crashers. He should have left such details to his personal aides.

But Edward had long since developed an innate cautiousness. Because he had remained anonymous over the years, the press and the public had become unimaginably curious about every facet of his life. After a carefully monitored childhood and an adulthood swathed in mystery, Edward had become fully aware of the dangers inherent in being part of such a wealthy family. Moreover, he'd been trained to handle the responsibilities his family, his money and his corporate enterprises demanded. He'd learned how attitudes and impressions could be swayed by greed.

Was it too much to ask for Edward to be allowed some normalcy in his life? The ability to eat fast food if he wanted, attend the symphony or ballet, or travel without a horde of reporters following his every move?

Edward took a deep breath to ease the tension settling in his gut and glared at his reflection in the mirror.

If he thought having his own identity discovered would create a media three-ring circus, imagine what the tabloid reporters would make of Edward Babcock spending the night with a woman who now claimed to be Princess Anushka?

Whirling, Edward reached for his bedside phone and punched the appropriate code for the security office.

"Rafferty here."

Edward didn't bother to identify himself. He merely said, "I want our near-drowning victim's things searched for identification."

"Already done, sir. I had my men go through her belongings as they were unpacked. We didn't find any names, addresses or personal data of any kind."

Edward worried his lower lip with an index finger.

"Is there a problem, sir? Do you suspect the

name she's given you is false?'' the disembodied voice asked.

"She hasn't given me a name yet," Edward said, hedging.

Not a real name.

The silence on the other end grew taut.

"I have reason to believe she might be suffering from some of the aftereffects of the accident Doc warned us about.''

"So we don't know *who* she is?" Rafferty slowly inquired.

"Not a clue."

The man sighed. "I'll see what I can find out with a quick, subtle interrogation of the guests.''

ANUSHKA TAPPED A TOE on the ornate Aubusson rug and glanced at the gold bedside clock for the fifth time in as many minutes.

What on earth was keeping Boris? He'd never bothered to keep his wardrobe in another room before. Nor had he ever taken so long to dress. Indeed, she'd become accustomed to having the man sleep on the floor at her bedside and accompany her nearly every waking moment. She couldn't believe he'd simply disappeared.

A chill coursed through her veins. What if something had happened to him? What if he'd been besieged by the very men they'd come to find? Naturally, Boris could be stunningly brutal, if forced to defend her, but he hadn't been himself this morning—so vague, so jumpy.

Her eyes narrowed, and she paced to the spot where he'd sat drinking his coffee. Coffee? Boris always drank tea—a particularly noxious brew mixed in his hometown of St. Petersburg.

Suspiciously, she sniffed the cup, then touched her finger to the last remaining drop, tasting it with the tip of her tongue. Despite her training, she detected no odor or taste of a telltale ingredient that could account for the change in Boris's demeanor.

Replacing the cup, she snatched her gloves and pocketbook from the top drawer of the bureau. Time was slipping through their grasp. If Boris didn't appear soon, she would be forced to make her way downstairs without him.

Filling her purse with the necessities—lipstick, compact, comb—she frowned again, wondering what had happened to the tiny derringer she always carried with her. Had Boris hidden it somewhere? Or had she lost it during her dunk in the ocean?

The door opened, and she whirled to confront her bodyguard.

"Where's the gun?" she demanded imperiously.

Boris's eyes narrowed to slits. "What gun?"

"My derringer. You know I never leave home without placing it in my purse."

"You didn't have it with you when you arrived."

"Damn." She tried to concentrate, but for some reason, the previous day's events were hazy, as if she'd sampled too much wine.

Of course! That was why her head ached abominably. She'd had too much champagne on the launch during their crossing. Then there had been cocktails at lunch, a dram of rum in her tea at breakfast...

"It's got to be here, somewhere," she said, gesturing to indicate the belongings that had been neatly unpacked and arranged in her current accommodations. "I want you to find it as soon as you can."

Boris didn't answer—not that she'd expected him to do so. He was generally taciturn, especially when he was in one of his surly moods or suffering from a hangover.

Some of the tension eased from her shoulders. Evidently Boris had sampled too much champagne, as well.

"Are you ready?" she inquired, moving toward the door.

"For what?"

"For our little adventure. My goodness, Boris. You are having such a hard time keeping up this morning."

He was watching her carefully. Too carefully. The alcohol he'd consumed must have given him a splitting headache, as well.

"I think you'd better go over our plan one more time," he finally said.

She stepped closer, needlessly smoothed the front of his shirt, then arranged the boiled collar and silk tie. For some odd reason, her heart thudded sluggishly in her breast and her mouth became unaccountably dry. His body heat was burning through the delicate fabric of her favorite Chanel, and yet gooseflesh had pebbled her skin.

"You really must stick to vodka, Boris. The champagne we had yesterday is affecting your memory."

"What's the plan, Princess?" he asked again.

In an effort to calm her fluttering pulse, she offered him a coy pout.

"I won't say another word until you call me Anushka," she said chidingly. "We're alone at the moment, so there is no need to be so formal."

He shifted, holding her with both of his hands. Broad, firm, masculine hands, with fingers that were long and sensitive and brushed with a smattering of dark hair. She'd often teased him that his hands were those of an artist, not a soldier. But then again, he'd often insisted that warfare was an art form all its own.

"What are you planning..." he repeated, then added, "...Anushka?"

She flashed him a flirtatious smile before she realized that such feminine wiles had little effect on this man. He couldn't be manipulated so easily. He had a will of iron, and nothing could tempt him from his sworn duty to protect her.

"I told you. We've been sent here to set a trap for MEOW."

"We're looking for cats?"

"Not cats, Boris. Cat burglars. Their association is known by the initials *M-E-O-W*. MEOW."

"MEOW," he repeated. "What does that stand for?"

"I don't know. I intercepted a transmission on the wireless—"

"The wireless?"

"You know, the small radio hidden in my flat in Moscow. Anyhow, I heard the ringleader of the thieves—"

"What thieves?"

"Boris," she said in a chastising tone. "You really must pay more attention. Either that, or you must refrain from drinking champagne in the future." Wriggling free, she placed the back of her hand against his brow. "Maybe you're ill."

"What about the thieves, Anushka?"

A frisson of alarm shuddered through her frame at Boris's continued ignorance. "We've been sent here by the Czarina herself to apprehend the thieves responsible for attempting to steal the crown jewels."

"What crown jewels?"

"The Czarina's," Anushka retorted heatedly. "Honestly, Boris, I fear you're losing your grip on reality."

"I don't think *I'm* the one with the problem," he mumbled.

When she would have retorted, he waved her rejoinder away. "So tell me, how do you plan to find these supposed thieves?"

"I believe they will be here at the gala. All of our sources tend to support that fact. The Czarina gave me one of her jewelry cases, as well as a hand-picked selection of precious gems. You and I will mingle with the guests, make our presence known, then do our best to convince everyone that we have become lovers.''

His eyes had narrowed again, an odd burning light appearing in their depths. The hand that still gripped her elbow pulled Anushka irresistibly closer.

"How do you propose we do that?" he asked silkily.

She snorted in disbelief. "Surely your injury didn't affect your memory of better days, Boris. You were once a man—"

"*Once* a ma—"

"A *man's* man. The rumors of your paramours still keep the Cossacks warm."

"You don't say..."

Her free hand slid beneath the hem of his jacket, curving around his waist, drawing him irresistibly closer.

"Don't tell me that the scent of my perfume doesn't fill you with longing. I cannot believe that you have forgotten what it is like to have a woman crushed against you." She flattened herself against the hard planes of his body. "I cannot believe you don't remember how a lover's kiss once filled you with awe and power." Lifting on tiptoe, she whispered, "I simply cannot believe it."

Then her lips were touching his, igniting a burst

of passion deep in her belly. Moaning, she shifted closer, pulling his head down to hers.

His body remained stiff and unresponsive for several seconds. Then, as if a dam had burst, he swept his arms around her waist and crushed her to him as if there were no tomorrow. She could almost have believed she had the power to arouse him.

Triumphant, she opened her mouth to his insistent demands for more. She moaned as his tongue swept over the barrier of her teeth to explore her intimately, savagely. All thought fled from her brain, all caution deserted her. For this single moment, she was merely a woman. And Boris was a man.

A man who couldn't...

You know.

Wrenching free, she put several steps between them, leaning against a small table for support.

Some distant part of her recognized that she had been well and truly kissed, by a master. She doubted that a shred of lipstick remained—and she knew she'd need to retouch her hair and reposition her hat. But she didn't care.

"Heavens, Boris." She sighed. "I never dreamed that you could still...or that you would even want to..." Sucking air into her lungs, she attempted to calm herself and prevent her tongue from babbling any further.

"Well," she said again, sweeping the cloche from her head. Turning, she regarded her reflection in the mirror backing the ornate deco étagère. She was a wreck, just as she'd suspected, but that wasn't what caught her attention the most. No, it was the heightened flush in her cheeks and the feverish sparkle to her eyes.

No. Oh, no. She would not allow a mere kiss to put foolish ideas in her head. After all, this man was her employee, her bodyguard. He knew her most intimate secrets and her worst faults. But she couldn't grow fond of him in any way other than that of a friend. To do so would ruin the special relationship they already shared.

"Yes...I..." she stammered, then forcefully continued. "I see that you have forgotten nothing from your rather lurid past. It shouldn't be difficult to make people believe our charade of mutual, undying love. That way, when you offer me the ring—"

"What ring?"

"The Czarina's. The one with the ten carat diamond."

"Ten carats!"

"Yes. And as soon as the MEOW members see it on my finger, it should only be a matter of time before they make a move to steal it."

She reset her cloche, applied her lipstick, then tucked the bag under her arm.

"Let's join the others."

"Where?"

She huffed in irritation. "Downstairs."

When she would have brushed past him, he caught her again. A jolt of sensation shot up her arm, but she ignored the reaction, firmly regarding Boris instead.

"Is something wrong?"

He opened his mouth. Then, obviously having reconsidered what he'd been about to say, he muttered, "This way."

To her infinite amazement, Boris touched one of the gilt sconces and a hidden panel slid free in the wall.

Anushka stared at the yawning aperture in amazement, then clapped her hands in delight. "A secret passage? Oh, Boris, how marvelous! You really are a wizard."

After pausing to brush a kiss against his cheek, she stepped into the void.

Chapter Four

Edward wasn't sure why he had revealed one of Babcock Mansion's secret passageways. He tried to tell himself that he didn't want to be seen coming from the private wing—especially with a woman so obviously confused about herself. But as he followed her through the dim, musty tunnel, a part of him whispered that there was some other reason for his motives. Something beyond being curious about this stranger's condition. Something far more than his obsession with being the knight in shining armor to every princess in distress. His mother had always accused him of bringing home every stray he encountered. This stranger was merely one more on a long list of such escapades.

Deftly leading the woman through a maze of intersecting corridors, Edward saw to it that they emerged on the outskirts of the garden. A door, which had been hidden near the corner of the house, opened a crack, and they were able to slip into the obscurity of a clump of lilac bushes.

"How in the world did you find these passages, Boris?" the woman calling herself Anushka asked.

Edward scrambled to find a logical answer. "I leaned against one of the doors last night, and the latch broke. When I tumbled into the inner corridor, I did some exploring."

Her grin was triumphant. "How very clever of you. This way, if anyone happens to see us emerge, they'll think we've retreated into the privacy of the trees for a tryst."

Edward fought to breathe at the thought of "trysting" with this woman in his mother's garden.

They crept past the lilacs and emerged in a wonderland of foliage. Edward's mother had been born in England—a charwoman who had fallen in love with an American businessman. Although she had willingly uprooted herself from her homeland, she had never been able to satisfy her craving for green things and roses.

"How lovely," Anushka murmured as she stopped on one of the split-rock paths. "The Czarina would love to visit such a place."

"Perhaps you should invite her to the party," Edward said, for want of something else to offer.

"Mmm. I would like that—*she* would like that. But the situation is far too dangerous for Her Royal Highness."

"MEOW," he inserted.

"Exactly."

Edward scanned the guests gathering in the garden. This morning, the gala festivities would commence with a treasure hunt. At ten, the guests would be paired off, then given the impossible task of finding a list of objects Dickerson had compiled. The event had been planned to allow the attendees an opportunity to whet their curiosity about Babcock Mansion—within reason, of course. The private wing and the security bungalow would remain off-limits.

Spying Doc Little conversing with a plump elderly woman—Greta Peery, Edward remembered from the guest biographies—Edward began steering Anushka in that direction.

"What are you doing?" she whispered dramatically, her lips barely moving.

"I...see someone suspicious."

The woman's eyes widened, and she became even more alert.

"Oh? Who?"

"That man." He pointed to Doc Little and watched Anushka, wanting to see if she would recognize the man who had examined her. If she remembered the older gentleman, he might be able to nudge her recollection of the accident.

But for all intents and purposes, he saw no recognition, no start of alarm. Nothing but the sparkle of intrigue.

"Why do you think he could be one of our suspects?"

Edward continued to watch her. He felt compelled to help her recall her true identity, but he didn't want to tax the limits of her endurance. "He claims to be a doctor."

"Oh, really," she drawled. "He doesn't look clever enough to be a doctor."

Edward tamped down a snort of spontaneous laughter, then disguised his unwilling humor with the dire pronouncement. "No. He doesn't."

Anushka reached for Edward's hand and forcibly wrapped his arm around her waist. Then she plastered herself against his side, making him much too aware of the delicate fabrics used to design her clothing.

"Remember, Boris," she reminded him sotto voce. "We should look like lovers."

"Of course."

Edward eased her toward Doc Little even more insistently. He couldn't help thinking she possessed a childlike and ingenuous quality—much like the fictional Princess Anushka. He found himself wanting to like her, to listen to her, to touch her...

No. Such emotions were dangerous. He couldn't possibly allow himself to confuse her even more— no matter how warm and exotic-smelling this woman might be.

The moment they reached the portly Doc Little and his elderly companion, Edward stopped. Unfortunately, Anushka used the opportunity to press even tighter against his side. One small hand, clad in a rust-colored kid glove, rested on the spot just above his navel.

Edward sucked in a deep breath.

Anushka pressed even tighter against his side.

Damn it all to hell. He *had* to get the doctor alone for some medical advice.

Greta Peery forestalled any such attempts by reaching for Anushka's hand and squeezing it as if the two women were long-lost friends.

"My dear," she said with a sigh. "How are you this morning?"

"I am quite well," Anushka said, one brow lifting in displeasure. Evidently, she thought that because she was "royalty," the woman should not have taken her hand. Edward had read somewhere that touching royalty was simply not allowed, and Anushka probably thought such familiarities went beyond the pale.

"Sweet child," Greta continued, unabashed. "When I saw you fall, I thought I would suffer some sort of attack myself." She clutched the region above her heart, drawing attention to a rayon dress of indeterminate age and style.

Edward fought the urge to growl in frustration. Great. He would have to guard over yet another weak constitution.

"I was so worried that my chatter was partially responsible for your accident. I should have left you to yourself, but I babbled on and on and on about my book and didn't give you a moment's peace."

Anushka regarded the woman with the same expression she might have given a particularly bothersome peasant.

Sensing the tension, Doc Little quickly asked, "And how is my patient this morning?"

Edward tried to catch Doc Little's eyes in order to convey that something was amiss, but the doctor continued to smile vaguely. Finally, at a loss as to how he should explain, Edward said pointedly, "Ask her."

The doctor turned to Anushka, his eyes twinkling beneath bushy brows. "Well, m'dear? How are you?"

Her chin tilted ever so slightly. "Am I to assume that you are speaking to me?"

The doctor shifted, clearly unnerved by her response.

"Yes, of course."

"And you think that I am one of *your* patients?"

He was still clinging to his good humor. "Not willingly, perhaps. But when you were brought to me like a half-drowned kitten, I took the liberty of examining you."

Anushka gasped, clutching the jacket of her dress together as if she wore nothing underneath.

"You *touched* me?"

Edward's lips twitched when he realized that Doc Little was emotionally floundering—much the same way Edward had been when this woman insisted on calling him Boris.

"I can assure you that there was nothing untoward in my—"

"Why didn't you call for my regular physician?"

Doc Little stammered, "I—I didn't have that information, nor did I think it necessary, considering that your vital signs were—''

"You took my *vital signs?*" she demanded, clearly horrified. "Do you mean to tell me that you listened to my heart?"

"Y-yes."

"That you touched my...bosom?"

Doc Little's cheeks filled with a ruddy color. "Only with my stethoscope, I can assure you." He pointed to Edward. "This man—"

"Boris," Edward supplied.

"Boris?" Doc's eyes widened even more as he grappled with the situation. It was clear that Dickerson had already informed him that Edward's name for the weekend would be Peter Falkland, and the change in plans had tripped him up.

"This man...Boris...can attest that I did not stray beyond the most cursory examination."

"He's right, you know," Edward said, throwing the man a verbal lifeline.

Regretfully, the comment caused Anushka to direct her anger at Edward. "Then *you* are responsible for this breach of protocol?"

"I thought it prudent to—"

"Prudent? *Prudent?*"

Her chin wobbled and her face crumpled. "Oh, Boris, how could you?" she cried, clearly distraught.

Edward stammered, sensing he owed her an apology. But even as the words were being formed in his brain, a choked cry was pushed from her lips, and Edward could have sworn he saw tears. Before he could think of a way to defuse the situation, the stranger turned on her toes and ran in the direction of the privet maze.

Her departure was marked by a stunned silence.

"What the hell?" Doc mumbled.

"Is she well?" Greta breathed. "She wasn't at all that…unsettled on the boat yesterday."

In an instant, Edward was reminded of the fact that this woman had met Anushka "ante-accident."

"Miss…"

"Mrs." Greta inserted. "Greta Peery. Please call me Greta."

"I'm Boris—" since Edward couldn't remember the stranger having mentioned a surname, and the only alternative that sprang to mind was Karloff, he refrained from supplying one. "Just Boris."

"How intriguing," Greta murmured, her cheeks adopting an odd flush.

Sensing he had unknowingly stumbled on a clue, Edward prompted the woman to verbalize her thoughts by saying, "Oh, really? Why?"

"Just yesterday, on the boat, that young woman and I—"

"You don't know her name?"

Greta shook her head. "We never formally introduced ourselves. But just before her accident, I was telling her all about the book I was reading."

"Which book?"

"Mistress of Moscow."

Another Princess Anushka fan? Coincidence?

"The protagonist in the book is Princess Anushka, and she has a bodyguard named Boris. In the novel, a suspected ring of assassins makes an attempt on the Czarina's life."

Although he tried to resist the tickle of alarm forming in the pit of his stomach, Edward found himself asking, "They don't try to steal her jewels?"

Had the woman somehow heard the plot of Greta Peery's book and confused that life with her own?

"Oh, no. I believe the attempt on the crown jewels occurs in *Princess for a Diamond*."

Edward felt a jump of excitement. "And the group was known as MEOW?"

"Nooo…" Her forehead wrinkled. "I don't remember anything called MEOW. But there was an instance when Anushka intercepted a radio transmission by Mia Wow, a notorious spy."

So the stranger must be an ardent follower of the Anushka books, judging by the way she'd jumbled several plots together.

"Thank you, Greta. Your information has been invaluable."

"I don't know how."

Edward glanced at the doctor, then realized that Greta Peery could only help the situation.

"The woman you just encountered is slightly… confused this morning."

This time, it was Doc Little who appeared concerned. "What do you mean, 'confused'?"

"She thinks she's Princess Anushka, and that I'm Boris, her bodyguard."

Greta gasped.

The doctor scowled.

Edward immediately asked Greta, "Did she tell you anything? About herself, I mean."

Greta's eyes bounced from Edward to the doctor. "I thought the two of you were...you know..."

Edward realized that his arrival with Anushka plastered against his side had indeed given the woman the impression of his being Anushka's partner.

"No, I'm afraid I've never met her before, either."

"Ohhh..." It was obvious that Greta found the whole situation intriguing. But then she was immediately worried. "Poor dear. How awful to forget one's identity, especially since she was so ill during the crossing."

"Ill?" This time it was Doc Little who spoke.

"Yes." Greta divided her gaze equally between the two men. "She was seasick. Horribly seasick. I don't think I've ever seen anyone that particular shade of green. That's why I was chattering on and on about Princess Anushka and her bodyguard. I thought I could help the poor child forget the troubles of her stomach."

Edward squeezed his eyes shut and rubbed at the ache beginning to settle in his skull. He was supposed to be finding explanations for his unexpected guest, but the situation was merely growing more and more complicated.

"Mrs. Peery? Could you excuse the doctor and I for a few moments? I need to speak to him privately."

Greta patted his arm. "Of course. I can see that you aren't well yourself."

Maybe that was the explanation for this whole bizarre situation, Edward decided. Maybe everyone else was sane and *he* was the one losing his grip on reality.

Still clucking, Greta made her way to a table resplendent with juices, coffee and morning pastries.

"What's wrong, Ed—er, I mean...*Boris?*" the doctor asked, quickly correcting himself. Then he leaned close to murmur, "You'd better tell that limey butler of yours about this unexpected change in plans. He's already told the staff to call you Peter Falkland."

Edward sighed. "I *will* be Peter Falkland. This whole scenario is a misunderstanding. As soon as I can explain to our guest—"

"No, no! You mustn't!" The doctor gripped his arm. "If what you've said is true, our guest will need to be treated with utmost care. Evidently, she's suffered far more than some incidental memory loss."

Edward grunted when a very real pounding began behind his eyes.

"Damn it, boy. Are you getting another one of your migraines?"

Edward automatically reached for the small pill-box that he kept close at hand, chose one of the tiny white disks and swallowed it dry.

"I don't think so," he said. Edward had suffered from migraines for as long as he could remember, but the dull throbbing in his head was completely removed from the blinding sensation that usually accompanied the malady. Nevertheless, the medication should ward off the pain.

"If you're not getting a migraine, then what's wrong?" Doc demanded.

Edward waved an arm in the general direction of the maze again. "It's that woman, this situation. I keep thinking her insistence on being Anushka is too weird to be true."

Doc Little shook his head. "I'm very sure that is *exactly* who she believes herself to be. You heard Greta. Our mystery guest was ill on the way over to Babcock Island, and she'd been listening to a plot from Analee Adler's book." He shrugged. "Add the trauma of her accident and a concussion to her preexisting condition…"

"She was seasick, not insane."

"Hear me out, Boris," the doctor said chidingly, then grinned. "Boris. The name suits you. So dark and forbidding."

"Out with it, Doc."

He chortled with glee, then wrapped his arms around his rotund belly and rocked back and forth on his heels. "As I was saying, the woman wasn't feeling well. She's been regaled with Princess

Anushka stories. She leans over the railing of the launch—perhaps to…relieve her stomach of its contents," he said delicately. "The blast of the horn startles her. She tries to right herself, but the boat bumps against the pier, and *whoosh!* She flies into the water."

"I'm well aware of that part of the story. I was there, remember?"

"Exactly. And you told me yourself that she hit her head at least once, maybe more than that."

"So?" Edward's eyes narrowed. "Are you trying to tell me we're trapped in some 'Gilligan's Island' amnesia sketch?"

"You've seen that one, too? I just love the way Mary Ann—"

"Doc!"

Doc snickered and ceased his rocking. "I doubt we have a case of true amnesia with this woman," he said. "I'd be willing to bet it's more of an instance of…mistaken identity."

"You're not making any sense."

"I'm making perfect sense. You heard what Greta said. Our guest was extremely ill during the journey. Before the trip ended, she had also suffered from a head injury and a near-drowning. Any of those events taken singly could cause the body to settle into a survival mode. Taken together, it's no wonder that her brain decided it was time to take a break from reality."

"Are you telling me she's nuts?" Edward drawled.

Doc laughed. "All I'm saying is that the woman is suffering from a mild case of bewilderment. I believe that her body is still coming to terms with the traumas it suffered. Give her some time and she'll remember who she is, how she got here, and every embarrassing moment she's had since."

"What if she doesn't get better?" Edward demanded. "She might have been a fruitcake from the very beginning. For all we know, she could be behaving as she normally does."

Doc Little's laughter increased, and he slapped Edward on the back. "Don't worry. I trust my instincts on this one. But if it will make you feel any better, if she doesn't snap out of this condition in a day or two—"

"A day or two! I thought you said—"

"Give it time, boy. The body is an amazing thing. It knows exactly what it can endure, and it will protect itself much more than we could ever believe possible. In the meantime, have some fun."

"*Fun?*"

"She looks like a nice woman."

"She could be a reporter, for all we know."

"Doubt it. She doesn't have that sneaky got-to-get-a-picture-of-that-Babcock-guy look."

"No, she's just off her rocker and thinks she's Russian royalty."

"So? There's no harm in that. Anushka is a fictional character, you said as much yourself."

"Yes, but *this* Anushka thinks I'm her trusty Russian bodyguard."

Doc's eyes twinkled. "Ironic, isn't it?"

Edward had been about to speak again, but the doctor's evident amusement sidetracked him.

"What's so damn funny?"

Doc grinned. "Here you are, with a beautiful creature hanging on your arm—quite literally—and you're complaining."

"Damn it, Doc," Edward muttered when an overdressed couple meandered close. "She wants us to appear as if we're having an affair."

"Oh, my..." The doc sighed with mock regret, and held a hand to his heart. "I *do* feel sorry for you."

Edward shot the man his most scathing look, but Doc was already warming up to his current theme.

"I can't imagine anything worse than having a charming, sexy..."

"Completely insane—"

"...desirable woman wanting to hold your hand, embrace you, perhaps even kiss you."

Realizing that he would get no help—or sympathy—from the physician, Edward threw up his hands in defeat. "Fine. Fine! I'll play along with the whole charade. I'll be Boris to her Anushka. But—" he speared a finger in the air "—she'd better be fully recovered in the forty-eight hours you promised, or I'm sending her straight to a mental-care facility."

Doc Little's features grew grave. "I'm afraid that you must do more than 'play along,' my boy. It is vital that our, er...princess feel completely safe in the role that her mind has chosen for her. If she were to receive any sort of shock, she could possibly sink even more deeply into a survival mode.'' He touched Edward's arm. ''I cannot emphasize this point enough. This woman must *be* Princess Anushka, and you must be a damned convincing Boris. We must do everything in our power to ensure that, for her sake, this island and its inhabitants give every impression of being from the early part of this century.''

''That shouldn't be too hard, given the request for period costumes for the gala.''

''And Anushka's presence could be written into the whodunit festivities to avoid questions from the other attendees,'' Doc Little suggested.

Edward sighed. ''Then I suppose I should inform Dickerson of our pretty little princess's condition.''

Doc Little grinned slyly. ''So I'm not the only one who thinks she's pretty?'' he prompted. ''You think so, too, don't you?''

Edward frowned.

''Come on, boy. I delivered you into this world. You can't hide anything from the first adult to paddle your backside.''

''Doc—''

''Personally, I'd say she's perfect for you.''

Edward didn't want to surrender to his own curiosity, but he couldn't help asking, ''Why?''

''Because you tramp around the real world with a fictitious name, concealing your true identity.

Now you've encountered a woman who—through no fault of her own—is in the same situation.''

"Doc—"

"Moreover," he went on, interrupting, "for the first time in years, you can toy with a relationship without having to worry that your significant other…"

"She is not my significant other—"

"…is dating you merely for your money."

"What the hell?"

"Don't you see? She doesn't have an inkling of who you really are. She is conversing and interacting with you as a man. A simple, ordinary man."

"She thinks I'm Boris," Edward drawled.

"And what is Boris, really?"

Edward sighed. "I don't know. I've never read the books."

Doc Little looked shocked. "You've never bothered to read your publishing house's most lucrative author?"

"I don't have a lot of free time."

"Then you'd better find some."

"Why? So I can be Boris through and through?"

"No. So you'll know what to expect."

"I hardly see why I should arm myself with a complete biography of the man, if she's bound to return to normal within a few days."

"Suit yourself," Doc said with a smirk. "Frankly, I think Anushka was quite wise in selecting you to be her sidekick. After all, the similarities are there. You could easily pass for a dark, forbidding Russian. Your skirmishes in business are much like his experiences in battle. And you've both been wounded.''

"What are you talking about?" Edward grumbled. "I've never been wounded."

"Ah, but you have. As a little boy, you suffered a horrible kidnapping ordeal."

"I was only two years old," Edward reminded him. "I have less than a half-dozen hazy memories of the event."

"True, but your mind remembers." Doc Little tapped his temples. "When the stress becomes too much, your brain uses its *own* survival technique and sends you to bed with a migraine."

"That's preposterous."

"Is it?" Doc Little's gaze became that of a physician studying his patient. "You've lived in a prison your whole life, Edward."

"You're getting maudlin."

"No, I'm telling you the truth. Your parents were so traumatized by your kidnapping that they enclosed you in a wall of anonymity. In some ways, they were very wise to do such a thing. You've been able to enjoy friends and situations without having your money get in the way. On the other hand, you've never had a chance to claim who you really are, the accomplishments you've engineered. Worse than that, you've never allowed yourself the opportunity to get close to a woman."

"I've been preoccupied with business the last few years."

"Yes, you have. But, that's no excuse for refusing to fall in love."

"And I suppose that Boris has suffered through the same slings and arrows of outrageous fortune?"

"Yes..." the doctor drawled. "Although he once had a reputation of being a ladies' man."

"I suppose Anushka helped mend his ways."

"Yes and no," the doctor answered, clearly hedging. Then he chuckled again. "She helped him recover from a horrible war wound, but even so, he could never...you know..."

"No. I don't know," Edward retorted sharply.

Doc grinned. "That's right. You haven't read the books." His laughter became a full-fledged snicker. "This whole situation should prove very entertaining. Very entertaining, indeed."

Before Edward could drill him for more information, Doc waved and moved to join Greta Peery.

Chapter Five

Edward found Anushka seated on a marble bench in the center of the maze. He supposed he should have been surprised she'd found her way through the tricky arrangement of hedges in such a short space of time, but he was beginning to believe that nothing this woman did could startle him.

Unfortunately, he realized how wrong he could be when she spun to face him and he caught sight of the tears brimming her lashes.

His stomach clenched, and he approached her with the same care he might give a wild animal about to bolt.

He was only a few feet away when Anushka sprang to her feet and exclaimed, "Boris, how could you? How could you have allowed that man to...to...touch me?"

Play along, Doc Little had said. Become Boris for her.

Sighing, Edward realized he had no choice. If he intended to unravel the riddle of this woman's identity, he would have to become part of her world.

"The doctor was correct, Anushka. He merely conducted a cursory examination."

"But, Boris!" she cried. "You consider him to be one of our suspects."

Edward had forgotten that he'd convinced her to approach Doc Little by claiming the man looked suspicious.

"When you fell from the launch and had to be revived, Anushka, I was worried about your safety."

"I had to be revived?"

"Yes."

"By whom?"

"By...me."

She waited expectantly for something more, so he added, "You'd had a terrible accident..."

She still waited.

"And I was desperately worried."

"How desperately, Boris?"

"More than words can describe." When she didn't respond, he added dramatically, "My life without you would have been desolate."

That comment must have put him over the top of the current hurdle, because she rushed into his arms and hugged him close.

"Oh, Boris, Boris! Will you ever be able to get over me?"

When he inadvertently snorted, she pulled free and placed her fingers over his lips. "No. Don't say it. Don't voice the words which should never be exchanged between us. If you do, our relationship would alter, and I couldn't bear such a thing, my dear, dear Boris.''

Once again, Edward had the sensation of being plunged into a play to which he'd never been given his lines.

As quickly as her anguish had appeared, Anushka brightened. ''So what activities have been planned for this morning?''

A bit taken aback by her sudden change in manner, Edward scrambled to remember that Babcock Mansion was filled with guests who had been promised a fortnight of entertainment.

''A treasure hunt will begin in—'' He glanced at his watch and scowled. ''Right now,'' he amended.

''A treasure hunt,'' Anushka repeated with near-reverence. ''How perfect. We can mingle with the rest of the group and begin gathering clues.''

''Won't they think it suspicious if we're trailing them instead of searching for the required items?''

Anushka patted his cheek as if he were an adorable child. ''Of course they would. That's why we shall participate in the game. Indeed, I plan to win the event.''

''Win?''

''Why not? After all, I'm very experienced in the detective techniques required, don't you think?''

She didn't wait for an answer. Taking his hand, she began pulling him through the maze, making her way closer and closer to the next improbable scene involving Princess Anushka and her cohort, Boris.

SINCE Edward had spent most of last evening tending to a wounded damsel, Dickerson had appointed Captain Hobbs master of ceremonies instead of introducing "Peter Falkland" as an assistant to Edward Babcock. Now the captain reluctantly took his place on the old granite carriage block, which served as an impromptu dais.

Hobbs caught sight of Edward just as the man raised his hands for silence. Edward grinned when the older man shot him a look that clearly pleaded for help. But since there was no way for Edward to assume his duties, the captain was forced to press on.

"Ladies and gentlemen."

The murmur of the crowd continued unabated.

"Ladies and gentlemen!" he said, more loudly.

No one paid him any mind.

A shrill whistle pierced the early-morning silence, and Edward caught sight of the ever-prudish Dickerson lowering his hand from where it had been poised in front of his mouth to make the sound.

At long last, the guests turned to Hobbs, and he cleared his throat. "I'd like to welcome all of you—" he made an awkward wave with his hand "—to the festivities. I regret to inform you that Mr. Babcock was detained…and has found it necessary to put me in charge of today's treasure hunt."

"I'm beginning to believe that Babcock fellow doesn't exist," a voice protested from the audience.

"I can assure you that he sends his regrets." The captain's cheeks were growing ruddy from his un-

accustomed role as public speaker. Taking a handkerchief from his pocket, he dabbed at the sweat
beading his brow. "Mr. Babcock hopes to join all
of you as soon as possible."

Edward caught the slight intonation given to the
word *soon*.

"In the meantime, he has asked me to welcome
you and give an overview of the day's activities."

A smattering of applause caused the captain to
halt, sputter, then wave uncomfortably.

"First, may I remind you that you are free to
roam the grounds, the beach and the mansion itself,
save for the security bungalow and the private east
wing. A few members of Mr. Babcock's security
team will be posted at these off-limits locations to
keep you from inadvertently straying."

"More likely, they plan to prevent us from getting within fifty feet of our host," one woman commented under her breath.

"Your generosity in contributing to the Children's Literacy Fund is greatly appreciated, and Mr.
Babcock has done everything in his power to make
this an event you won't forget. If there is anything—*anything*—you need, please ask for that gentleman there."

Hobbs pointed to Dickerson, who in turn glared
at the captain for his improvisation.

"Dickerson, if you would be so kind as to dis-
tribute the treasure-hunt lists."

The stiff-backed butler began circulating among
the guests, passing out the vellum instruction sheets.

"Since this is a get-acquainted activity, you are asked to choose a partner whom you don't already know," the captain added. "Try to find someone smart." He laughed weakly at his own joke, then rushed to add, "All right, everyone, find your partners."

When Anushka tried to move, Edward snapped a hand around her waist and pulled her tightly against him. Heaven only knew, he couldn't have her approaching some stranger and introducing herself as Princess Anushka before any of the whodunit scenarios had even been presented.

"Boris," she protested.

"We're supposed to be lovers," he reminded her. "Our ruse will appear more genuine if we break the rules a little."

"I suppose," she agreed reluctantly. "Even so, I'd like to have a chance to plumb the depths of a suspect's mind."

"We don't have any suspects yet."

"Everyone is a suspect."

When Edward didn't release her, she added, "I promise to choose someone who appears fairly devious, if you wish."

Great. That was all he needed. Princess Anushka drawing a life story from some wealthy and influential guest, then accusing him or her of being part of the dreaded MEOW gang.

"I thought you wanted to win this game," he said.

"I do."

"Then we stick together."

"If you insist."

"I do."

Her brows rose at his imperious manner, but she didn't argue.

"Ladies and gentlemen." Captain Hobbs waited for the crowd's silence.

Dickerson passed by Edward, handing one of the vellum lists to Anushka. She began to peruse it, her brow wrinkling in concentration.

"What you have in your hands is the first clue to the game. If you solve the riddle correctly, you will be led to the next clue, and the next. The team to reach the treasure first may keep whatever they find. But be forewarned," Hobbs added quickly, "as in any whodunit, there are red herrings, false clues and dummy treasures waiting to be discovered, as well."

Hobbs looked at his watch. "You have until six o'clock to complete your mission. In the meantime, a buffet will be laid out in the dining hall to appease any hunger pains you might endure. At the appointed time, we will all rendezvous here, in the garden. Make sure that you bring your treasures with you. And may the best man—or woman—win."

As Captain Hobbs stepped from the carriage block, his audience abandoned all pretense of ignoring the papers in their hands. Soon the murmur of voices and the squeals of laughter filled the sea-spiced air.

"You read it, Boris," Anushka said, handing him the paper.

"Very well."

Since Dickerson had devised this particular game, Edward was as ignorant as the rest of the guests as to what "treasures" might be tucked away on the estate.

"'I am harsh, but ever fair. Hundreds fear my hundreds, but by exercising caution, my face will reflect approval. What was gained will be lost. What was lost will be gained.'"

Edward watched Anushka's nose wrinkle with intense concentration and, not for the first time, he found himself staring at the woman. What a conglomeration of contrasts. A woman who was forceful, yet demure. Feminine, yet bold. Strong, yet vulnerable.

Sane, yet loony? his conscience supplied unbidden, and he scowled.

"'I am harsh but ever fair,'" she repeated. Turning in a slow circle, she surveyed the estate from all angles. Harsh things...harsh things..." she thought aloud. "Boris, what do you see that could be considered harsh?"

For the first time in as long as he could remember, Edward found himself studying the estate with utmost concentration. As he surveyed the rolling lawns, the bountiful garden and the stern but inviting facade of the mansion, he was struck suddenly by the beauty that surrounded him.

When had he stopped seeing this place? When

had the fairy-tale magic of his boyhood haunts been replaced by grown-up worries about business?

"Well?"

He cleared his throat. "There are several things that could be considered harsh. The house, the sea, the brambles on that bush over there."

He pointed to a spot in the garden where two couples were already inspecting the area.

"No..." Anushka drawled. "I think it's something else. Something much more subtle." She took the paper. "'Hundreds fear my hundreds.'" She sighed, clearly perplexed. "'But by exercising caution, my face...'"

Her brow furrowed in concentration, and she slapped the paper against her palm.

"Come along, Boris. Since most of the guests appear to be searching outside, let's look in the manor house for some sort of inspiration."

ANUSHKA'S BRAIN WHIRLED as they stepped into the foyer.

"Harsh...harsh..." she murmured to herself, her eyes scanning the rooms open to her view.

Taking Boris's hand, she hurried to the stairs.

"Where are we going?" he asked.

"Upstairs."

"Why?"

"Before we can safely hunt for the clue, we have to allay suspicion."

"Suspicion of what?"

She headed quickly up the stairs, pausing only

long enough to shoot him a wry smile. "Come now, Boris. Do you honestly think we aren't being watched? Anyone with half a brain would have to know that this treasure hunt is child's play for us. If they wanted an advantage, they would only need to follow us."

"Don't you think you're being paranoid?"

"Not at all. I call it common sense."

They had reached the top of the landing to the second floor. Searching the elegant sitting room that ran from the staircase to the rear of the house, she noted the priceless Louis XIV furniture, the sparkling wall of windows leading out to the terrace and the gilt ornamentation bisecting the pristine white walls.

"How very cliché," she commented under her breath.

Boris stiffened beside her. "What's cliché?"

"This room," she said with a sweep of her hand. "It has been decorated in *nouveau riche* meets Louis XIV. How trite, how boring."

For some reason, Boris grew even more poker-faced than usual.

"I don't see anything wrong with it. It's a very elegant style."

"Yes, of course. If a person chooses to be a lamb of fashion, diligently following the tried-and-true traditions of French aristocrats who lost their heads two hundred years ago." She sniffed. "But the Babcocks aren't royalty. Royalty would know better. *I* would know better."

"And what would you have done with this room?"

She peered at it with narrowed eyes, envisioning how she would redecorate, were she the mistress of this establishment.

"I would paint the walls red. A deep ruby red."

"What?"

Since it was clear that Boris didn't share her vision, she explained. "This room is a jewel in and of itself—look at those windows, the architecture, the fretwork of gilt. None of that is noticed because the drama of the surroundings have been dimmed by fussy, nobody-wants-to-sit-in-it furniture. In red, a person would feel energized and compelled to stay. Yes, I think red is the very thing needed here. Personally, I adore red."

"Maybe it's the Russian in you."

She would have retorted tartly, but at that moment, she heard footsteps on the stairs. "Quick!" she whispered, then pulled Boris into an alcove displaying the smooth, muscular form of a Rodin nude. Grabbing Boris by the lapels, she pulled his head down and pressed her lips against his own.

Just as before, a jolt of pure sexual energy shot through her body at that tiny point of contact. Her arms wrapped around his neck, and she clung to him, kissing him as she had never kissed before.

No man had ever held her like this. No man had ever caused her to fear that her heart would leap from her breast with its pounding. She was on fire, inside and out. But instead of being consumed by the heat, she found herself wanting more and more.

At that same instant, Boris's body lost its customary stiffness, and he bent to her more completely, his lips slanting over hers, his tongue bidding her enter. He pushed her against the wall, his hard chest crushing her, embedding the imprint of his studs in her skin.

From somewhere far away, she heard a giggle, a whispered comment, but she didn't care. There was only this moment, this man. Her fingers splayed wide and she tested the musculature of the man who kissed her, noting the rippling strength of his back, his shoulders, his abdomen. Like a blind woman, she read his body with a hunger unlike anything she'd ever known.

Unlike anything she'd ever known...

No, that wasn't quite true. There had been other men. Princess Anushka was known for her lovers.

Lovers? What lovers?

She whimpered slightly, unable to think through the haze of passion. Obviously misunderstanding her moan, Boris allowed his lips to stray from hers and began exploring the sensitive skin beneath her chin, the array of nerve endings hidden in the arch of her neck.

Think. Think.

About what? She couldn't remember anything but this moment. This man.

When at long last Boris drew back, they were both breathing like long-distance runners finishing a marathon. She stared up at him, seeing a face she didn't recognize.

When had Boris's hair begun to adopt those careless waves? When had his eyes become that brilliant shade of blue? And when had the planes and angles of his face become so well-defined that they could have been hewn from a piece of marble?

"They're gone," he murmured.

She felt the words begin as a rumbling beneath her fingers.

"Who?"

"The people who followed us."

"Oh."

She couldn't bring her scattered wits together enough to move. There was something amiss here, something dreadfully wrong, but she was afraid to move, for fear that the sensual spell would be broken.

"So what's the answer to the riddle? What are we looking for?"

She stared at him, wondering what twist of fate had brought him into her life. It had to be something dramatic and...

Oh, yes.

The war.

That blasted, dirty war.

The war that had changed him forever, wounded him emotionally and physically and robbed him of his ability to...

You know.

Don't think about what happened. Don't think

about the seriousness of his wounds, his delirium, his thrashing. When he finally awakened, he'd lost so much weight that...

Weight?

"A scale," she whispered as she wriggled free of the barrier of his arms he'd made when he leaned against the wall. Unfortunately, as she disengaged herself, her breasts rubbed against his sleeve, and it was Boris's turn to look distracted.

"What?"

"The answer to the riddle is a scale. A bathroom scale. 'I am harsh, but ever fair,'" she quoted. "A scale harshly tells the truth, but is fair because it will not lie. 'Hundreds fear my hundreds...'" She was finally regaining her wits again, her poise, her confidence. "Lots of people fear the numbers, which usually read in the hundreds."

Boris took over. "'But by exercising caution, my face will reflect approval.' An obvious reference to losing weight."

"Exactly. As are the lines 'What was gained will be lost...' meaning shedding the extra pounds. And 'What was lost will be gained'—a note about one's health improving."

"Come on."

This time, Boris took her hand, leading her from the sitting room to a wide corridor interspersed with doors. Stopping at an elaborate man-size baroque clock, he touched a portion of the molding on the wall and the timepiece slid to one side, revealing yet another secret passage.

"Boris!" she exclaimed in delight. "However did you know it was there?"

"A hunch."

She followed him into the dim interior, sucking in her breath when he leaned against her to pull the secret door shut again.

"Is something wrong?" he asked, his shadow looming above her.

"No. No, what could possibly be wrong?" she responded, her voice too bright, too breathless, too...needy.

"You gasped."

"A...spider," she lied.

He did not move away as he was supposed to do. Instead, his shoulders loomed over her in the shadows, big and dark and strong. The kind of shoulders a woman could lean upon, cry upon, confess...

What could she possibly want to confess?

"I wouldn't have thought that Princess Anushka would be afraid of spiders."

"Oh, yes...I...I abhor them."

"Then you must tell me when you see one."

"Oh?"

"I would gladly kill for you, Princess. Slay whatever dragons—or spiders—you wish."

She tried to laugh at his joke, but the sound that emerged was more of a choked sob.

Boris's hand touched her cheek, and she jumped.

"What's wrong, Anushka?"

"I'm fine."

"Liar. Your body is trembling."

She bit her lip, suddenly overwhelmed by a wave of confusion and disorientation. "I don't know... I..."

Once again, he wrapped her in his arms, but this time, the overriding emotion that he brought with his embrace was a curious gentleness and empathy.

"Is it so very frightening? Being in the dark?" he murmured, tucking her head beneath his chin.

She was amazed at how well they fit together, how well his body shielded hers from real and imagined dangers.

"Yes." She wasn't sure how the word emerged from her throat. Never in her life had she admitted to anyone that there were times when she felt afraid. "I hate not knowing..."

The words trailed away.

"What, Anushka? You hate not knowing what?"

Her brow creased as she tried to remember her original thought. She couldn't account for the way she'd grown so scatterbrained of late. Maybe it was the accident and the bump to her head. Ever since she awakened, nothing had seemed right.

When she didn't speak, Boris brushed his lips against the top of her head, and she squeezed her eyes shut at the inestimable joy the gesture brought to her heart.

"Don't try to think about anything, Princess," he whispered. "Everything will come to you in its own good time."

"Will it?" she asked, her voice small in the blackness of the passage. She couldn't account for the wave of loneliness and regret that threatened to overwhelm her.

''I promise,'' he answered solemnly.

''Well, then...'' She gently removed herself from his hold, knowing that if she didn't put some space between them she would never think clearly again. ''I suppose we should find that scale.''

She tried her best to inject a note of haughtiness into her tone, but she merely sounded bossy.

Behind her, Boris laughed. ''Very well, Your Royalness. Follow me.''

Chapter Six

Twenty minutes later, Edward approached Dickerson and handed him a beribboned magnum of Dom Perignon, 1927.

For the first time in his career at Babcock Mansion, Dickerson's mouth gaped, and he stared at the champagne in disbelief.

"How d-did you possibly... You didn't help with any... The clues were..."

"Princess Anushka found it," Edward said with a grin.

"But, sir," Dickerson protested, "I specifically made up dozens and dozens of nearly incomprehensible hints to keep the guests busy for hours."

"Maybe you and the princess think in the same diabolical way."

Dickerson didn't seem at all pleased with such a prospect. "Princess Anushka. Harrumph."

Obviously, Doc Little had spread the word about their stranger's condition. Dickerson seemed downright insulted that the woman had dared to impersonate one of his own favorite literary characters.

Even so, his shoulders resumed their proud line, and he asked, "What shall I do about the other guests?"

"Put another bottle of champagne in the final hiding place. No doubt someone else will stumble on the treasure sooner or later. As for this—" he tapped the Dom Perignon "—have it chilled for later."

For the second time in as many minutes, Dickerson's jaw dropped. "Chilled, sir?"

Laughing, Edward sauntered away from the butler, making his way to the study, where he'd left Anushka. "You heard me correctly the first time, Dickerson. There's no need for me to repeat what I said."

As Edward made his way up one of the back staircases that led to the east wing, he marveled at the fun he'd had so far that day. Fun. When was the last time that such a word had been used in connection with his life? He honestly couldn't remember. Somehow, he'd become imprisoned by work, duty and the responsibilities of his family. He'd forgotten that a person sometimes had to break away from his routine and add some whimsy to a dull existence. It had taken a woman with a mistaken identity to remind him of such a thing.

Reaching the third floor, Edward moved to the door leading into the garret bedroom. Long ago, the cavernous space had been converted into a children's playroom. Since Anushka insisted on watching the other guests, he'd suggested they survey their "suspects" from a distance.

In truth, he'd meant to keep Anushka away from the gathering as much as possible. After their first kiss in the sitting room, he'd sensed a different mood in the woman. One that wasn't quite so confident. One that was...

Vulnerable.

Yes, that was it. She'd become less of a bother and more of a real person to him. He hadn't wanted her mind to suddenly clear of its current farce in the presence of so many people.

Slipping into the playroom, he stood for a few minutes in the shadows clinging to the sloped ceiling and corner fireplace. Opposite, Anushka was seated on the floor, in front of a child's piano. To his amazement, she was actually picking out the melody to *Rhapsody in Blue*—a piece of music written well after Princess Anushka was supposed to have lived.

"That's pretty," he said quietly, not wanting to startle her.

But the surprise was his, when it became apparent that she'd been aware of his entrance from the very beginning.

"Where have you been all this time?" she asked casually, too casually, her fingers altering their path and beginning the "Maple Leaf Rag."

"I took the champagne to that butler fellow and asked him to chill it for us."

"'Us?'" she drawled.

"I thought we might drink it later as a celebration."

"What are we celebrating?" She seemed intent on the tiny piano keys, but he knew from the electricity in the room that her mind was on their conversation.

"A job well done. The swift conclusion of the treasure hunt."

"The treasure hunt is nothing more than a game. There are larger things at stake here."

"Such as what?"

"A band of thieves. The safety of the Czarina's jewels."

He allowed that particular subject to wash over them. Moving to the gabled windows, he planted his hands on either side of the sash and stared down at the guests who were scurrying around the grounds like ants at a picnic. Their gaily colored costumes, period hairstyles and outrageous mannerisms almost made him believe that he had been transported to another time and place.

Almost.

The *plinkety-plink* of the piano stopped, and Anushka stepped behind him, standing so close to him he could feel her breath against his shoulder.

"This house is very surreal in many ways," she murmured.

"How so?"

"There's a peace here that is unlike anything I've ever known."

"And what else have you known?"

She grew incredibly still, then moved against

him, as if to leave. He caught her hands, forcing her to stay. "What else have you known?" he repeated.

"Noise," she said after a long pause. "Lots and lots of noise. I—"

A shrill scream split the somnolent afternoon, and both Edward and Anushka rushed to flatten themselves against the glass.

An elderly woman clutched at her neck, lifted her face to the sky and screamed again.

"What in the world?" Edward muttered.

Then Anushka brushed past him, urging, "Hurry, hurry! Something is dreadfully wrong!"

Edward managed to pass Anushka on her way down the unfamiliar staircase in the secret corridor. Shouting instructions about which door she should take, he burst outside and ran to the rear croquet grounds, where a crowd was already gathering.

"Help me, help me!" the elderly woman continued to scream, her clawlike hands clutching her throat. "Someone has stolen my jewels."

Jewels?

Edward skidded to a halt, still several yards from the knot of people gathering around the stricken woman. His gaze slid over the onlookers, becoming aware of two things simultaneously. First, there wasn't a single security guard in sight, and second, Dickerson was watching the proceedings from the vantage point of a small knoll.

"Damn it," Edward whispered to himself, altering his course so that he could approach Dickerson under the guise of bracing his foot on a retaining wall and tying his shoe.

"Am I to understand that this woman is one of the actresses you hired?" Edward inquired under his breath.

Dickerson continued to focus on the distraught woman and her audience, giving no outward clue that he and the man known as Boris were even conversing.

"Yes, sir. You asked me to organize a whodunit for the fortnight."

Edward sighed, his head bowing in defeat. "So you chose a caper?"

"Naturally. What could be more fun than a thief running amok? Especially with this crowd."

Lifting a hand, Edward rubbed his brow. "I wish you'd warned me."

"Whatever for, sir? You generally have no tolerance for party preparations."

"That's true. But our unknown guest already thinks she's the infamous Princess Anushka, hot on the trail of a ring of jewelry thieves."

"I beg your pardon?"

"You heard me. She's so confused about her own identity that she thinks a notorious gang of thieves—known only as MEOW—has come here to steal the Czarina's jewels."

When Dickerson didn't respond, Edward chanced a quick glance in the butler's direction. Dickerson's eyes had taken on a glassy sheen of disbelief.

"Oh dear," he murmured.

Over the din, Edward heard Princess Anushka taking charge, bidding the other guests to move back, grilling the elderly woman concerning the supposed theft. Within moments, Edward was sure that Princess Anushka would identify herself.

He could only pray that the rest of the gala attendees would think she was part of the show.

ANUSHKA THREW OPEN the door to her suite in the east wing and strode inside, her gait triumphant.

"Didn't I tell you that MEOW would strike?" she asked her bodyguard. "My instincts were straight on, I tell you."

"Mmm."

She didn't bother to chide Boris for his less-than-enthusiastic response. There was very little time left before dinner, and she would have to change in record time.

Sweeping the cloche off her head, she tossed it on the couch, then ran her fingers through her hair. "I could use one of your infamous massages, Boris. I feel like a bundle of nerves. But there isn't time, you know. Dinner is set to be served soon."

"Not for two hours," he said, sinking onto the settee and propping his feet on the coffee table.

"Exactly. Barely enough time for me to appear my best."

His brows rose. "You need more than two hours?"

She wagged a finger in his direction. "Now, Boris, don't be a spoilsport. You know my ritual."

Anushka slipped her jacket from her shoulders, allowing it to puddle on the floor. Boris was constantly scolding her for such habits, but since he invariably organized the room after her, she saw no need to change.

"I'll take a bath first. Will you ring for some rose petals, lemon peel and vodka, please?"

"Excuse me?"

"Rose petals, lemon peel and vodka. I'm sure the kitchen could round up such simple ingredients."

"Don't you think you should save your drinking until after dinner?"

She laughed, wondering when Boris had become so witty. He generally didn't tease her this way.

"Oh, Boris, you are a prince." Unable to still her delight at his inexplicable carefree manner today, she ran toward him and kissed his cheek. Then, bending at the waist, she extended her arms in front of her. "Help me out of this thing, will you?"

Boris didn't respond, so she peered at him beneath the fringe of her bangs. "Take my hem, Boris. You know this gown is all but impossible to get out of on my own."

Finally, he complied with her orders, holding her hem and allowing her to wriggle out of the dress backward—as if she were some sort of butterfly shedding her cocoon. Sighing in delight at the cool kiss of air, she kicked her pumps off and padded toward the armoire.

"What should I wear this evening?"

Boris didn't answer. He was still holding her

dress, his gaze bouncing from his hands, to her shoes, to her underwear-clad body.

She sighed, reaching for one of the hangers. "Which one, Boris? The Erté—" she held up an exotic blue-satin gown trimmed with fringe "—or the Schiaparelli?"

Her bodyguard cleared his throat, opened his mouth, then coughed again. "Whatever you'd like will be fine."

She sighed. "Sometimes I wish you could be less of a man, Boris," she stated regretfully. "You really don't seem to understand the important role fashion plays in the struggle for power."

Eyeing each dress, she replaced the Schiaparelli and threw the vibrant Erté on her bed. Opening one of the lingerie drawers, she chose a teddy made of the finest Chinese silk and adorned with ribbon and lace as fragile as a cobweb.

Sinking onto the bed, she unhooked one of her garters and began to roll a silk stocking to her ankle.

"The constant war between men and women has to be carefully planned—and a woman's only arsenal is her body, her poise and her brain."

She draped one stocking over the corner of the bed and bent to remove the second. "I would have thought that you—a soldier—would understand perfectly."

"Anushka…"

Ignoring his protest, she continued, "Of course, I suppose that you didn't bother to ponder such things before your accident made you... You know."

"What do I know?"

She threw him a pitying glance. "Really, Boris. Don't make me be cruel."

Standing, she made her way into the bathroom. "Give the kitchen a call while I draw the bathwater. Just this once, I'll do it myself."

THE DOOR SLAMMED behind her, but not before Edward caught sight of her delicate hands unhooking her brassiere. The same one he'd been asked to fasten only that morning.

Wrenching his eyes away from the panels of the bathroom door, he glanced down at the dress he held, then tossed the garment on the settee, as if it would spontaneously combust.

Just when he thought he had a handle on this woman, the vulnerability he'd seen had disappeared and she'd been transformed into the queen of Sheba, Salome and Mata Hari all in one.

Sighing, he raked his fingers through his hair and squeezed his eyes shut. Damn, damn, *damn,* how had he ever stumbled into this bizarre scenario?

"Boris?" her voice called from the bath. "Have you made the call?"

"Have I made the call?" he muttered to himself. "I ought to be making a call to Bellevue, that's what I ought to do."

He reached for the phone, but before his fingers made contact, a knocking came from the hall.

Stomping to the door, he whipped it open to reveal the dour Dickerson holding a tray. Upon it lay a crystal bowl of rose petals—freshly picked, judging by the heady scent—three gleaming lemons, a tiny nutmeg grater, a bucket of ice and a bottle of vodka.

Edward stared at the items in amazement. "How did you know that—"

Dickerson brushed past him. "I've read the books, sir. Everyone knows Princess Anushka's regime."

"Everyone but me," Edward muttered.

One of Dickerson's brows rose as he set the tray on a small table.

"You haven't read the novels?"

"No, I haven't. And I seem to be the only person on this island who hasn't."

"I'd wager you were correct in that assumption, sir."

"Have we got any?"

"Any what, sir?"

"Any of those Princess Anushka novels?"

"I've already donated mine to the library, sir. On my day off. Last week. They can't buy enough of those books for the demand they have."

Edward planted his hands on his hips, resigned to the fact that Her Worthiness wasn't going to return to her original self this evening. Due to the circumstances, he'd be better off if he at least knew his own role in this *théatre royal*.

"What about the rest of the staff?"

"No, sir. My book was circulated through the household and security people before I gave it away."

"That's a pretty popular book."

"Indeed, sir."

Sighing in defeat, Edward offered, "I suppose we could ask the guests—that Peery woman had one on the boat."

"It might prove awkward to inquire, sir, since the guests now believe that Princess Anushka is part of our whodunit sketch. Only Mrs. Peery is aware of Anushka's…condition. Even so, asking for her book might cause her to think something is seriously wrong with our unknown guest."

Edward scowled. "Then get Captain Hobbs to send one of his men in a launch to the mainland. Tell him to buy all of the Analee Adler novels he can find and bring them back here immediately."

Edward wasn't sure, but he thought Dickerson's lips twitched in a slight smirk.

"Very well, sir. Will there be anything else?"

"No," Edward snapped.

Dickerson was halfway to the door when Edward changed his mind. "I take that back. Tell him to bring some ice cream, as well."

This time, Dickerson's eyes sparkled with hidden glee. "Baskin Robbins hand-packed chocolate-chocolate fudge?"

"You know what I like, so don't bother to ask."

The butler actually offered a fleeting smile. "My, you must be in a dither. You haven't sent someone to the mainland for ice cream, in say...three or four months.''

Edward glared, and he suddenly wished that Dickerson hadn't worked on Babcock Island since before his birth. That way, the stodgy British gent wouldn't know that Edward had learned at his mother's knee to chase away the tension of an oncoming headache with hand-packed ice cream and warm, straight-from-the-oven chocolate-chip cookies.

Dickerson must have read his thoughts, because he murmured, ''I'll have the chef begin the cookies right away.''

Edward opened his mouth to offer a pithy retort, then gave up the notion. What could he possibly say?

''Oh, and sir,'' Dickerson offered, poking his head around the door, ''you'd better start warming up those creative juices of yours. Because of Princess Anushka's involvement in the whodunit performance this afternoon, the script we'd originally intended to use will have to be abandoned. The actors asked to have the new text first thing tomorrow morning, so that they can begin memorizing their lines.''

Edward was sure that he heard Dickerson's laughter floating down the hall behind him. Growling in frustration, he plunged his hand into the ice bucket, selected a fistful of cubes, and held them against his forehead.

But, to his intense surprise, despite the tension of the day, his head didn't ache at all.

Chapter Seven

Dinner was an extravagant affair. All the guests were seated at an enormous seventeenth-century dining table with an inlaid design of a peacock made from a dozen shades of hardwood. The china was vintage Spode, the porcelain prewar Japanese, the crystal Waterford. An ice sculpture of a swan about to take flight dominated the center of a large floral bouquet, while a chandelier imported from France shed a thousand bits of rainbowed light over damask Irish linen. Even the wealthiest participants were surprised and delighted at the measures that had been taken to impress them.

The only person who didn't gaze wide-eyed at the elaborate display was Edward. He only had eyes for Anushka.

She was beautiful. Absolutely beautiful.

Never in his life had Edward seen a woman with eyes so expressive. In the candlelight, they appeared even larger and darker. The silky bob of her hair enhanced the olive-colored irises, while marcel waves framed her face and made her skin seem that much paler. She'd lined her eyelids with kohl and painted her lips scarlet, the stark twenties-style makeup giving her the allure of a silent-screen starlet come to life. But the dress she wore...

She should be arrested for what it did to a man.

The gown glowed with blue fire, the cut exquisite—a simple shift style from shoulders to ankles. But from there, Erté had taken a mischievous slant on fashion. The décolletage was low, extremely low, allowing Edward to see the shadow between Anushka's small, firm breasts. And in back...

Well, the back was nonexistent, the plunging vee settling just below the curve of her waist. Long strands of fringe provided a mock sleeve over one arm. Then the black strands seemed to disappear in the draped sapphire fabric around her hips, before reappearing again at a slit that ran from hem to mid-thigh.

Edward hadn't been able to take his eyes off her all evening. The dress, her makeup, her hair, had provided a foil for her dramatic personality and vivacious sense of humor—and he'd noticed that he wasn't alone in his admiration. After introductions were made and those present assumed that Princess Anushka was part of the whodunit scenario, she had become the main point of attention. Quite cleverly, she'd grilled her ''suspects'' under the guise of polite small talk. Her methods were so subtle that Edward doubted the evening's participants knew what was happening.

Afterward, the floor to ceiling French doors leading to the patio had been flung open to the cool night air. A jazz band had assembled on the lawn, and several small tables with tea-light centerpieces had been arranged around an impromptu dance floor. Liveried servants waited with carafes of coffee and tea and trays of tiny pastries.

"Shall we?" Edward asked, bending low over Anushka's chair before another man could offer to escort her outside.

She offered him a smile that had the ability to jolt his pulse. Then she stroked his cheek in what he thought must be an unconsciously proprietary gesture.

"But of course, *mon ami.*"

When she would have taken a seat in the shadows, he pulled her resolutely toward the dance floor.

"Would you care to tango, Princess?"

For a brief moment, he thought he saw panic in her eyes, and he wondered if her true self had no knowledge of the steps required. But then she melted into position and followed his lead as the rich, primitive Latin beat stirred his pulse even more.

"You've had a busy evening," he murmured, bringing her body close, their cheeks together.

"Why would you say that?"

"I took careful note of the conversation."

At the far side of the patio, they both pivoted and began striding in the opposite direction. In the brief moment they were parted, he hadn't missed her coy smile of triumph.

"I've been able to deduce a great deal from the guests."

"Do tell."

"First of all, I'm sure that doctor is involved with something nefarious. You must watch him carefully."

"Of course."

"Then there's that Peery woman."

Edward made a mental note to have Dickerson speak with Greta again. The butler had already taken her aside once to explain the predicament with their mystery guest's condition, and she had willingly agreed to continue playing along with the ruse.

"Then there's that Babcock fellow."

Edward involuntarily stiffened.

"What about him?"

"Don't you find it odd that the man would organize such an elegant affair, then never show his face?"

Edward swung Anushka in a dip. Once upright, she continued uninterrupted.

"Granted, the man has a reputation for his eccentricities, but I still think his absolute inattention is strange."

"Perhaps he *is* here," Edward offered. "It's rumored the man likes to socialize incognito."

She sniffed in evident disdain. "If the man were here, I would have ferreted out his identity within twenty-four hours."

"How?"

"Quite simply. By studying the way the servants interacted with him, I would know him instantly. There would be an air of deference whenever he was near, no matter how well Babcock might have trained them."

Edward was stunned by her astuteness. He *had* trained his household staff well, and they *did* know to ignore him when company came to the island. But even Dickerson sometimes attended to Edward's comfort far more solicitously than he might that of an unknown businessman.

"Furthermore, I find the man's obscurity completely intolerable."

"As a child, he was kidnapped."

She shrugged her shoulders—those beautiful, pale shoulders—as if to say such a fact was inconsequential.

"That was forty years ago."

Edward couldn't help correcting her. "Thirty-six."

"Surely he's had time to come to terms with what happened."

"It must have been a horrifying experience."

"One of which he would have little, if any, recollection."

"That may be true, but I'm sure he was raised to fear another such event's happening. His parents probably transferred their own worry to him—unconsciously, of course."

"No, that's not it."

Edward clamped down an involuntary chuckle.

"I think," she continued, "that the man is silently crying out for help, but isn't secure enough in his own masculinity to actually do so. I think that he has repressed a good portion of his inner will. He's become a stand-in puppet for his father—a father whose ghost continues to lead him in a Machiavellian dance."

Well, that explanation was rather dramatic.

"Edward Babcock's father is still very much alive, and touring the world with Mrs. Babcock," he informed her.

"That's what everyone has been led to believe," Anushka insisted. "In reality, he is dead, buried, and torturing the son who could never please him— and I have proof."

"What proof?"

They had reached the end of the dance floor, and she stretched on tiptoe, making a ballerinalike sweep of her hand. "I heard one of the servants call my suite of rooms 'Mrs. Babcock's apartments.'"

Edward swept her into another dip, then said, "So?"

"So, don't you find it out of character for the original Babcocks—the man and woman who had only their utter devotion to cling to when their son was taken—to have separate rooms?"

"Perhaps Mrs. Babcock is recovering from, say…hip replacement surgery, and the man is merely being conscientious of his wife's comfort."

"No. That's not it at all. The man is dead, I tell you—*d-e-a-d.*"

It was Edward's turn to shrug. "Believe what you want, but I would have to be shown more proof than separate bedrooms."

Her eyes narrowed. "Are you challenging me, Boris?"

Edward opened his mouth, hesitated, then reconsidered his response. What would the "real" Boris do? He was Anushka's bodyguard, but did he generally take a subservient role?

"What do you think?" he finally said, unwilling to make any kind of declaration.

"I think you are," she murmured, still watching him closely. "And you know how I respond to such displays of Neanderthal-like domination."

The effect may have been a trick of the light, but he thought her eyes had begun to burn.

"Come with me," she ordered, pulling him from the crowded dance floor. She made her way into the house, padding from the dining hall to the main corridor, and from there to the first set of double doors.

Tugging him into the black shadows, she closed and locked the doors behind them. Then she grew silent—so silent that a frisson of goose bumps raced up his spine.

What had he done? Had he offended her? Was she about to show him who was master of this particular duo?

Damn it, what if Anushka had completed some sort of martial-arts training? Was he about to be thrown to the floor and mauled?

Anushka threw herself against him, and Edward

automatically wrapped his arms around her torso in an effort to control her. But when her lips crashed over his own, and she began to kiss him with the insistence of a long-lost lover, he forgot everything but the heat of her body, the sweetness of her kiss.

Somehow, in the darkness, he managed to bump his way through his father's old study, locating the leather couch in the center of the room. His body was on fire as he sank into the cushions, and Anushka flattened herself over him, her hands ripping at the studs of his shirt.

Summoning every ounce of control he possessed, Edward wrenched free, took her by the shoulders and forced her to sit—keeping a foot of space between them.

"What the hell?" he gasped, trying to gather his equilibrium.

Her breathing was as ragged as his own. "You know I can't stand to be ordered about like a lackey," she huffed.

"And *this* is the way you punish a man?"

There was a beat of silence, and he reached for the lamp he knew would be on the side table. Flicking the switch to the lowest setting, he found himself staring at a very rumpled, very sexy, very intriguing Princess Anushka.

She self-consciously smoothed her hair. "Well, no," she admitted somewhat sheepishly. "I had meant to chastise you—in private—but then…"

"But then?" he prompted when she looked at

him again, her eyes as dark as the bittersweet cocoa on his mother's favorite truffles.

"But then I suddenly couldn't keep my hands off you. Call it a...Freudian slip of some sort."

Freud. Didn't the man connect all deviant behavior to a lack of sex?

Without conscious thought, Edward reached for her, dragging her back into his arms. This time it was he who dominated, he who sought out her lips again and again.

She was like quicksilver in his arms—moving, shifting, her body rubbing against him in all sorts of delicious ways. He wanted to surrender to the moment. He wanted to pull this woman onto the floor and make love to her again and again and again.

But a tiny corner of his conscience still had the ability to warn him that this woman was ill. It wouldn't be right for him to seduce her. It wouldn't even be right if *she* seduced *him*.

"No!"

Breaking free, he jumped to his feet. "We can't do this," he insisted, raking his hands through his hair.

He made the mistake of looking at her. One of her dress straps had slid from her shoulder, revealing the plump shape of her breast nearly to the nipple.

Shuddering, he balled his hands into fists and strode to the ornate mahogany desk, leaning against it in an effort to displace the sexual energy thrumming through his veins.

"You're right," Anushka said. Then, more forcefully: "You're *right*. I had no business treating you so shabbily. I love and respect you more than any other friend on this earth. Our relationship is precious to me. I couldn't bear to see your feelings toward me change. Not after all we've been through, all we've…"

He glanced over his shoulder in time to see her hand wave through the air. It was another quirky gesture he had come to adore in this woman. When lost for words, she referred to the world around her, as if that mannerism were explanation enough.

"I also should have been more sensitive to your condition."

Turning, he leaned his hips on the desk. "My condition?"

"Your…" Her hand waved again, this time in his direction, and he felt his cheeks redden as he realized she must be referring to the arousal that was not quite disguised by the loose pleats of his tuxedo trousers. "I shouldn't have reminded you of your…wound."

Her last comment caused him to pause. "My wound?" he echoed.

She jumped to her feet, clearly agitated. "Don't make me say it, Boris. Don't make me remember those horrible hours."

Damn it, where were those books? And how

many of them was he going to have to read tonight to discover what she was talking about?

She rushed to him, grabbing fistfuls of his shirt, shaking him slightly. "Why do you torture yourself this way? Why do you torture me?"

He wasn't sure, but he thought a sparkle of tears shone in her eyes.

"You know very well that we can never make love."

"Why?" he asked gently, even as he told himself he should agree with such a declaration.

"Because you can't...you know."

"I can't what?"

She covered her face with her hands. "Don't make me say the words. Don't make me remember that moment when I found you, broken and bleeding, your life ready to slip through your fingers."

Then her head lifted, and she offered him a look so filled with hurt and accusation, he was stunned.

"I see. Now you intend to be the cruel one. You intend to remind me that it was my choice that we never made love? Damn it, Boris!" she cried, pummeling his chest with her small fists. "Must you show me how much my body yearns for your own? Just as it did in Paris?"

Paris? What happened in Paris?

"That night before you returned to the lines, I almost begged you to take me, but you insisted that we would not love one another until...we'd... wed."

Boris had promised to marry Anushka? Why did

that seem so atypical of a character created by Ana-lee Adler?

She choked on a sob.

"You were so cruel to her, Boris. They'd set a date, rented a hall. Her mother had even bought a dress!"

But even Edward knew that Anushka was reported to have been an orphan from infancy. And why was she suddenly referring to herself—or at least her "imagined" self—in the third person?

"She was so excited, so full of dreams. They'd even picked out a house together. She gave him her savings—her grandmother's inheritance—so that he could offer a down payment. Then he was off to the war and she never saw him or her money again."

He took her by the shoulders, realizing that this was not Anushka speaking, but the woman beneath the facade.

She continued, undaunted. "Stupid, stupid girl. It was only then that she woke up to discover that her prince in shining armor was nothing more than a frog. He'd lulled her into feeling safe with him. He took her money and her heart, then left her to realize how gullible she'd been. How naive."

She took a deep, ragged breath, and he supported her under her arms when she seemed to sag slightly. "She vowed that she would never love another man like that again. They're all liars. Liars and thieves. She swore she'd find a way to support herself—in a grand enough style that she could hoard each penny until she could afford to track him down and make him pay for what he'd done. She even took a job as a secretary—keeping her own talents hidden because the money was better than anything she'd find anywhere else.''

The woman jerked away from him, tipping her head to a proud angle. ''She is not an idiot or a victim. She knows exactly what kind of game her boss is playing, but she doesn't care. Soon she will have enough to hire a private investigator and re-claim her self-respect.'' She stabbed the air with her finger. ''Then she'll show the world that they've all been duped by the real princess of this fairy tale, just you wait and see.''

With that, she pivoted on her heel, took two steps, then froze. Looking up, she seemed to sway ever so slightly. Glancing behind him, Edward noted that her attention had been caught by the enormous head of the water buffalo Edward's great-grandfather had bagged on an African safari. The piece was old, musty and disheveled—no matter how many hours Dickerson spent vacuuming and combing the beast's mangy fur.

So why didn't she look away? Why was the color ebbing from her skin?

The animal wasn't important enough to warrant such concentration. There was nothing about it to frighten her. Nothing to make her open her mouth, scream as if she'd seen a terrifying apparition...

Edward jumped as the sound tore through the

quiet study. Then, just as quickly, the space became
quiet as the woman fainted dead away and crumpled
in a heap on the carpet.

Chapter Eight

Less than half a minute passed before the study door flew open and Doc Little, Captain Hobbs and Dickerson appeared in the yawning aperture. One look at their accusing expressions told Edward plainly enough that they blamed *him* for the present situation.

"What happened?" Doc Little demanded. Without waiting for an answer, he strode toward the princess and began to examine her supine shape.

"Nothing. Not a damned thing happened," Edward insisted. "She just...fainted."

Dickerson snorted in disbelief, sweeping a blanket from the sofa and draping it over her body, as if the room had taken on a sudden chill or the princess threatened to succumb to shock.

"Just fainted," he grumbled. "Women don't 'just faint.'"

"This one did."

"You must have done something to her."

"I didn't do anything! She looked up at the wall—"

"Edward Remington Babcock." Dickerson interrupted him, using the same no-nonsense tone he'd employed when Edward was small and slid down the newly polished banister or tracked mud into the foyer.

"Be honest, boy. What did you do to her?" Dickerson demanded, patting the princess's hand while Doc Little checked her pupils.

"I didn't do a blasted thing!" Edward insisted again. "We were having a discussion—"

"That must have been some discussion," Captain Hobbs muttered under his breath, flicking Edward's collar, his brow creasing in grandfatherly disapproval.

Too late, Edward realized that his pristine shirt was streaked with lipstick—as was his chest beneath.

As guilty as a schoolboy caught stealing penny candy, Edward tugged the shirt together and attempted to fasten it. When he realized that most of his studs lay scattered on the carpet, he gave up.

"All right, we shared a kiss," he admitted, as if these men were his parents and they'd demanded a confession.

"Looks like more than one to me," Hobbs observed.

"Okay. *Okay.* We kissed a few times."

"I'd say you did more than kiss," the captain continued.

"Damn it! I am nearly forty years old and your employer. I do not have to explain what happened between Anushka and I. We are both consenting adults.''

''You might be consenting adults, but when your partner screams and faints dead away, you can count on an interrogation,'' Little said sternly. But his eyes gave him away. They twinkled with suppressed mirth.

Edward took a deep, calming breath. ''We were dancing on the terrace. Something about my manner convinced Her Royal Fictitiousness here to bring me to the study for a private confrontation. The door shut, and—'' He halted, realizing he'd given more details than necessary.

''And what?'' Dickerson demanded. Of the three men, he was the only one still clinging to his usual dour civility. Somehow, in the space of a day, Dickerson had appointed himself protector of their unknown guest. With each hour she spent in his presence, the butler grew more and more concerned, clucking over her well-being like a mother hen with one of her chicks.

''She all but attacked me,'' Edward admitted reluctantly.

Doc guffawed.

Hobbs snickered.

Dickerson glared even more.

''I swear! She ran across the room, threw herself at me, and began kissing me.''

Dickerson's lips pursed. ''I can see that you put up a hell of a fight.''

''*Yes,*'' Edward said, emphasizing the word by

punching the air with his finger. "I tried to convince her to stop."

"Then what happened?" Doc Little demanded.

Edward felt his cheeks redden, and he damned the sensation. Good hell almighty, he was a grown man, one who was mature, sensible and experienced with women. So why did he feel like such a putz explaining his reactions to Princess-Whoever-She-Really-Was?

Maybe, just as she'd claimed, he *was* the wart-covered toad to this woman's beautiful princess.

"Well?" Little prompted.

"I...uh, kissed her back," Edward admitted guiltily.

Hobbs was openly laughing now.

Dickerson offered a shocked, "Sir! How could you?"

"Damn it, she's a very pretty lady—a *beautiful* lady. And that dress...it ought to be illegal." He lifted his hands in supplication, but only Dickerson appeared to be taking him seriously—and he definitely didn't approve.

"I broke away, though," Edward continued. "I told myself she was sick and I couldn't surrender to the...atmosphere."

"What atmosphere?" Hobbs said between huge belly laughs. "When we burst into the study, it was all but pitch-black in here."

Dickerson shot the captain a scathing look. "Then what happened, sir?"

"We talked."

"About what?" Little said as he covered his patient's shoulders with the blanket.

"About...psychology."

"Uh-huh," Little drawled.

"What sort of psychology?" Dickerson asked.

"Well, uh...something about Freud."

"Hey, Doc," Hobbs called. "Isn't he the guy who always talks about sex?"

"That's Dr. Ruth," Edward retorted before the man could head up the right alley.

"You still haven't told me anything that can account for this woman's condition," Doc Little inserted, changing the subject.

"I don't *know* what happened. She started talking about Boris, the war, and some secret wound."

When the men exchanged glances, Edward was sure that he was missing an important piece of the puzzle surrounding Princess Anushka.

"What?" he demanded impatiently.

None of the men answered.

"What the hell happened to Boris?"

"Boris isn't real, sir," Dickerson reminded him needlessly.

"I know that." He pointed to the woman on the floor. "But she thinks he is, and she thinks *I* am that man. You told me to play along with her delusions of grandeur, and I did. But I need more information about the man, if I'm to continue the charade any longer."

"Is that when she fainted?" Doc inquired.

"When the two of you were discussing your...er, rather, *Boris's* injury?"

Edward shifted, the scene replaying in his head. "Well...no. She began babbling about the way Boris was intent on stealing her money. Then she began speaking in the third person, and I sensed that she was offering me a tidbit of her past—this woman's *real* past."

"So *that* was the moment she fainted?"

"No...," Edward drawled, reluctant to add any more details. But when the men eyed him expectantly, he was forced to add, "She fainted just after she'd informed me that she'd saved nearly enough money to show the world they'd been duped."

"No," Dickerson said heatedly, clutching the woman's hand to his breast. "She hasn't duped anybody. She's ill. She injured herself while she was a passenger on *your* boat."

Edward sighed in frustration. "I know that, Dickerson. I was there, remember?"

The butler had the grace to look shamefaced. "My apologies, sir."

The doctor stood and brought the conversation back to the original point, his own tone filled with irritation. "So *that* was the moment she swooned?"

"No. She swooned after she saw the water buffalo."

The three men blinked at him as if he'd announced that a host of aliens would be joining them all for a nightcap. It was Dickerson who managed to speak first.

"I beg your pardon?"

"She fainted—" Edward repeated, enunciating each word "—when she caught sight of the water buffalo."

"Why?" Hobbs asked.

Edward threw up his hands. "How should I know?"

Hobbs shot him a quick look, one that clearly stated, *You're being unreasonable and you know it.* Turning to Dickerson, he offered, "Maybe she has a fear of large animals?"

Dickerson appeared to be giving the ridiculous comment more thought than Edward believed necessary.

"Or perhaps she was scared by a water buffalo as a child," he offered slowly.

"But she was orphaned at a young age. How could she have seen a water buffalo in Moscow?"

"Damn it, that woman is *not* Princess Anushka!" Edward shouted, then quickly controlled himself.

Closing his eyes, he concentrated on his breathing, on relaxing his muscles—even as he conceded that this woman had brought total chaos to his life. Before her accident, he had prided himself on being calm, rational and completely in control of himself. Even when his migraines struck, he didn't rail against the Fates. He identified the problem, took appropriate remedial measures, then allowed time to solve his worries.

But since diving into the ocean to reclaim this woman's body from the sea, he had been swamped with a dozen intense, and completely atypical, emotions—frustration, confusion, irritation, passion and protectiveness.

Opening his eyes again, he asked Doc Little, "What do *you* think is wrong with her?"

The doctor shrugged. "In my expert opinion, I'd say she fainted."

Edward held his breath, counted to ten, then clarified, "But what made her *faint?*"

Doc Little pressed his lips together in concentration. "I'd say the water buffalo startled her."

Again, Edward struggled to keep his voice even. "That's it?"

"Until she can tell us otherwise, that's my official opinion."

"Do you have an...unofficial opinion?" Edward urged, keeping his voice saccharine-smooth.

"I suppose." He hefted himself to his feet. "I would say that this woman has been under a great deal of stress lately. Her body is underweight, and her reaction to the water buffalo leads me to believe her nerves are finely wrought. In addition, when I turned her to listen to her lungs, I noted that the muscles in her shoulders and neck are knotted into lumps the size of golf balls. That kind of physical tension doesn't appear overnight."

"So you think that the stress she encountered before her accident has contributed to her...identity problems."

"I'd say her stress *caused* her current condition. Something has happened to her that she wishes to forget, and her body is allowing her just that opportunity.''

Edward studied the supine woman—the steady rise and fall of her chest, the lax appearance of the arm draped over her waist.

"Should we take her to the mainland?" he said, knowing that this time Doc Little would agree with the idea.

"I...don't know."

Edward glanced at the man in surprise.

"Other than her...mental irregularity, there's nothing physically wrong with her. A hospital couldn't provide anything more in the way of remedial services than what she is receiving here. Oh, sure, they'd send her straight to a psychiatrist, but I don't think that's necessarily the best course. From what I've seen, the woman has enjoyed her visit to Babcock Island. Her role as Princess Anushka has shielded her psyche from stress, and she has shown every indication of relaxing her mental guard. You said yourself that she gave you pieces of information that probably came from her real past. I think she'd be better off here. With us."

Dickerson continued to grip the princess's hands, but his eyes had adopted the bleak hopefulness of a cocker spaniel's. Hobbs's laughter had stilled, and his features pleaded with Edward to agree.

As if Edward really intended to *disagree.*

Nodding his head, Edward assumed the casual I-don't-give-a-damn expression he was accustomed to using with business associates. Even so, he couldn't ignore the way his own palms had grown clammy at the thought of sending Princess Anushka away.

"We'll give her a few more days."

His three friends visibly wilted in relief.

"In the meantime, I'll continue to play the part of Boris so that I can keep a close eye on her."

"What about the actors, sir?" Dickerson inquired, some of his British stiff-upper-lip demeanor returning.

"What about them?"

"They managed to include Princess Anushka in the middle of their first scene, but they have been unable to continue with the current script."

"I suppose I could help," Edward stated.

Dickerson shook his head. "You've admitted yourself that you haven't read the Anushka books."

Edward sighed, realizing that Princess Anushka had upset more than one carefully laid plan for the benefit gala.

"I'm delegating that responsibility to you, Hobbs."

"Me!" Hobbs splayed his hands over his chest.

"Yes. *You*. After tonight, I've become aware of your talents for comedy and drama. I would love to see what you can do with your theatrical gifts."

Hobbs sank into a chair, looking positively glum.

"As for you, Dickerson, you'll need to inform Greta Peery of this setback and obtain her continued willingness to play along."

"Gladly, sir."

"Doc, I want you to talk to Rafferty. Ask him if he's had any success in tracking down a name for our mystery guest."

"I'll see Rafferty right away."

"Good."

Calmer now, Edward moved to the couch and scooped Anushka into his arms. She groaned softly, then cuddled against him. Somehow, during the conversation being held around her, she'd slipped from a faint into an exhausted slumber.

"I'll take Her Loftiness upstairs to bed." When his companions' eyes narrowed, he clarified, "*Her* bed. Then she can spend the rest of the evening *alone*."

"Oh, no, sir. That won't do," Dickerson hastily objected. Edward's brows lifted, and Dickerson explained, "She thinks you are Boris. Boris always sleeps on the floor by her bed as part of his security measures."

Edward thought of the hard floor and the aches he'd suffered the night before. "I'll sleep on the couch. If I hear her stirring—"

"No, sir," Dickerson insisted. "You have to be there in case she wakes up and reaches for you. Your absence could be very upsetting."

Sighing, Edward silently conferred with the doctor. When the physician nodded in assent, Edward surrendered to the inevitable. "All right, but you'd better check on the launch we sent to the mainland. I'll be needing those Princess Anushka books to help me get some sleep."

SLEEP? he thought later. He hadn't been able to sleep at all.

Soon after he took Anushka to her suite, Dickerson had arrived with a shopping bag slung over his elbow. Inside the sack had been all fourteen of the Analee Adler novels. In addition, Dickerson had carried a tray with a plate of chocolate-chip cookies, a carafe of milk, a Baskin Robbins ice cream container and a crystal sherbet dish.

"Will there be anything else, sir?"

Edward had absently waved him away, already digging into the supply of books.

"No, thanks, Dickerson. Put our other guests to bed, then retire for the night yourself."

"Very good, sir."

The butler had padded to the hallway, then popped his head inside again just before he closed the door. "Hobbs asked me to beg you to change your mind about his working with the acting troupe."

Edward had grinned. "Tell him I'm so pleased with his eagerness to help. I'll expect a stunning scenario tomorrow at breakfast."

Dickerson's lips had twitched ever so slightly. "Yes, sir. I'll tell him." The door closed with the faintest of metallic snaps.

Now Edward automatically glanced at his patient, but she continued to sleep soundly. He'd removed her gown, hosiery, and shoes, then covered her with a sheet. To his amusement, the woman was sprawled across the middle of the bed, her mouth slightly open, her fingers twitching in apparent response to a dream.

Edward was quite sure that if he informed her in the morning of her nocturnal appearance, or the tiny moans and snatches of words she offered, she would be embarrassed to the core. She would probably bar "Boris" from ever sleeping at her bedside again.

But Edward found such complete abandon endearing—even adorable. So much so that for the past few minutes he'd found it hard to do anything but stare at her.

Keep your mind on the task at hand, Babcock, his conscience reminded him.

Ripping the lid of the ice cream carton free, he ignored the crystal dish and cradled the container in his lap. Using the silver spoon Dickerson had supplied, he began to skim the softer, melting ice cream from the edges. Absently he placed the dessert in his mouth, held it on his tongue for several seconds, like an expert wine taster, then finally swallowed and repeated the process.

Sifting through the books, he stacked them in the order they had been published and cracked the first cover. Unfortunately, he found the reading to be slow and slightly tedious, the narration stilted and the characterization weak. Then, remembering that someone had told him the first novel had met with only lukewarm success, he skimmed the rest of the story.

So far, he was less than impressed with what he'd found, he thought as he dropped the paperback on the floor. Indeed, he wondered how the manuscript had made its way past an editor's desk, let alone to the bestseller lists. Even if the book had developed a cult following, he couldn't imagine why Analee Adler's devotees were so rabidly loyal to the series. The plot had been somewhat interesting, but the whole spy, thriller angle had depended upon a host of clichés. Even the ending had left something to be desired, providing a wrap-up to the tale, but no real sense of justice.

So why had this stranger felt such an affinity with the Russian princess? Why, of all the people and characters her mind could have chosen to hide behind, had she selected this particular heroine?

Sighing, he picked up the second novel in the series, praying that Boris would at least make an appearance, so that his evening wouldn't have been an entire waste of time. And the moment he opened the second novel and read the first line...

He was hooked.

Chapter Nine

The first time I saw Boris, he wore the uniform of a Russian colonel.

Never in my life had I been so glad to see someone of my own nationality. I felt safer just looking his way. Yet at the same time, the mere sight of him caused a tremor of fear. He was so tall, so dark, so infinitely male, that he took my breath away. There was an aura of ruthlessness about him that could not be hidden. His eyes glittered in the overcrowded bistro, his lips were but a slash in a hard, craggy face. He had the look of a man who had paid dearly for the experiences of his past. Yet whatever hardships he had endured had not broken him. No, he had been tempered like fine steel.

Edward couldn't help a small grin of pleasure.

"Fine steel," Edward murmured under his breath. "Yeah, that sounds like me."

Skimming several pages, he found the passage that described the first meeting of the characters.

...in an instant, I knew that my life was at stake. If I didn't think of something quickly, Count Marino's men would close in on me like a swarm of barracudas.

Carefully regarding my surroundings, I discovered that the only two exits available to me had been blocked by the count's men. The windows were such that unless I charged through them, breaking the glass, they would offer no escape.

I was about to lose all heart when I saw him again. The Russian soldier. He tossed back the vodka remaining in his glass, then stood, fishing into his pocket to remove a few coins and toss them on the table.

I had no other choice. I would have to trust this man—this stranger—to help me.

Even as I weaved my way through the tables crowded with lovers, soldiers on leave and the usual assortment of underworld "businessmen" who frequented such a place, I knew that the man might well refuse to help me in any way. The fact that he was a Russian did not necessitate his compliance. In fact, as an officer in the cavalry, he might consider himself above "saving a maiden in distress."

Pushing forward as quickly as I could, I reached the man just as he was about to turn away. Grasping his elbow, I managed to turn the soldier toward me. Then, before he could speak, I threw my arms around his neck and cried, "Darling!"

Before he could react, I pulled him down for a kiss—the kiss of a lost soul, of a woman completely in love and doomed to lose her heartmate. Then, before he could wrench free and demand an explanation, I pressed my cheek close to his and whispered, "Please help me."

To his credit, the Russian didn't speak or push me aside. Instead, his arms wrapped around my waist—loosely at first, then more tightly when he felt the trembling of my body.

"Do you see the men positioned by the doorways?"

As a response, he dipped his head as if nuzzling my neck.

"*Da.*"

"They are trying to kill me."

His lips moved against my own in a way that could only mean he smiled.

"Why would anyone want to kill so lovely a creature?"

"Because I know too much about them."

"And what sorts of things do you know?"

I hesitated, aware that if I shared my secrets with the wrong person, I would pay for such information with my life.

"I have proof that they mean to assassinate the Czar."

The man grew inestimably still, but as his fingers dug into the flesh at my waist, I sensed that I had unknowingly stumbled upon an ally.

"Faint."

The low, gravelly tones of his voice were barely intelligible, and I frowned.

"What?"

"Faint."

Then, to spur me on, he nipped my earlobe.

I needed no more coaxing to follow his wishes. Indeed, when his teeth tugged at my flesh, my legs lost their strength and I sagged against him.

Without pause, the Russian called out, "Make way, make way! It's the fever!"

There had been enough of a panic of scarlet fever in the area to cause an immediate scattering of customers. In the midst of the melee, the Russian carried me up the narrow staircase to the cool evening air. Without pause, he made his way down the street in great, ground-eating strides.

Not daring to open my eyes, I lolled against him, feeling suddenly vulnerable. Unbidden, a knot formed in my chest, and I felt the rise of tears. It had been so long since anyone had held me, touched me, honestly cared for me.

I chided myself for losing my nerve, but with each step, the man reminded me over and over again that I might have developed a reputation for being a masterful spy...

But underneath the bravado, I was still a woman...

Edward grabbed a chocolate-chip cookie, his eyes riveted to the pages as the protagonist, who had failed to impress him in the first Analee Adler book, suddenly sprang to life. And as Boris entered the pages, the sexual tension became unbearable. When the bodyguard demanded a kiss of the infamous Princess Anushka as payment for his services, Edward couldn't have put the book down had his hair caught on fire.

So this was why the guests at his party had become so twitterpated the moment Princess Anushka had introduced herself? This was why the simple whodunit sketch had become that much more interesting and the participants more willing to play along. In this novel, Anushka became a woman with strength, humor, vulnerability and class. Boris, on the other hand, was cynical, world-weary, and cruel to everyone but the princess. With Anushka he showed a side of himself that was both protective and endearing, stern and sensitive.

The hours melted away. Edward barely noticed when Dickerson appeared to take his tray. He didn't even react when Dickerson proclaimed, "I wish you'd have a word with Hobbs, sir. Tonight, the whodunit script took a rather alarming turn."

"Sure, Dickerson, whatever," Edward mumbled

between the last few bites of his cookie. Whatever twinges of a headache he'd experienced earlier were no longer there. In fact, he found himself oddly energized.

"I could spell you for a while if you wish...in playing nursemaid, I mean."

"I put it on the tray."

From somewhere far away from the French trenches of World War I, Dickerson sighed impatiently.

Marking his spot with the end of his thumb, he glanced up at the man, blinked, then offered him an absentminded smile when Dickerson continued to glare at him.

"How was the whodunit tonight?" Edward asked in an effort to placate the man.

"As I stated earlier, sir," Dickerson said, enunciating each word with great care, "Hobbs has taken a rather wicked turn with the script."

"Oh? No more jewelry heists, I take it?"

"No, sir. He indicated that you'd left instructions that since Miss...er, the princess was under the impression that a ring of cat burglars was under our roof, you would prefer to alter the crime."

"Excellent. What did he decide to do?"

Dickerson looked pained. "He managed to bring Boris and Anushka into the plot to support our...uh, guest's confusion."

"Marvelous."

Edward began to return his attention to the book, but Dickerson interrupted him.

"No, sir. It isn't marvelous."

"Is something wrong?"

"Yes. Something is horribly, horribly wrong."

When Dickerson wrung his hands and appeared to be ready for a fit of apoplexy, Edward kept his finger between the pages and shut the book, giving the man his full attention. He couldn't ever remember the butler looking so nonplussed.

"How far have you read, sir?" Dickerson asked quickly.

Knowing that the butler was trying to delay some sort of embarrassing pronouncement, Edward stated simply, "Boris has been wounded, and Anushka has just found him in the hospital."

The butler's face suddenly radiated nostalgia. "Such a touching scene, a truly touching scene."

"Dickerson, we were speaking of Captain Hobbs and his newly found scriptwriting career."

"Yes, sir. I suppose we were," the butler whispered.

To Edward's complete surprise, a stain of color crept up the butler's cheeks. Never, in all the time he'd known the gentleman, had Edward seen him blush.

"Sir, I believe Hobbs has stepped beyond his bounds as a trusted employee. He has decided that our whodunit sketch will involve a murder."

In Edward's opinion, the idea didn't warrant such distress, so he prompted Dickerson. "Go on."

"Well, sir, he has decided that the corpse-to-be is to have a reputation for being a bit of a lothario.

He will be the one responsible for the attempted robbery, which has already been performed.''

''And...''

''And the man is to overtly woo and romance several women at once, within the full gaze of the guests.''

''I don't see a problem there.''

''But, sir, he has decided that *I* should be the roaming lothario.''

Edward automatically cracked a smile, and had to pretend to rub his mouth to avoid hurting the older man's feelings.

''Just who are you supposed to romance?''

Dickerson's cheeks grew scarlet.

''Mrs. Gardner-Smythe.''

Mrs. Gardner-Smythe was at least eighty years old, wore too much makeup and bangle-covered clothing, and was constantly taking cruises to the Bahamas so that she could watch the ''young stud muffins'' sun themselves on the beach.

''Who else?''

''Mary Wilson.''

Edward pressed his lips together in an effort to look offended. Mary Wilson was a fifty-five-year-old society maven with enough collagen added and plastic surgery done to her body to make her bounce.

''Is that all?''

''No. I am also supposed to have liaisons with Ethel, the downstairs maid, and that tartish actress Roxy Rollins.''

Hobbs was definitely taking his role as a writer seriously.

"You have your work cut out for you," Edward said, as steadily as he could—even though he was dying for Dickerson to leave so that he could have a good laugh.

"I am not a man of loose morals."

"Of course you aren't."

"If this whole event hadn't been for charity, I would have told the man to…to…go hang!"

"He is a rascal, isn't he?"

Dickerson's fists balled. "He's much more than a rascal, sir. He's a…a rounder, as well."

"I suppose you would like me to have a word with him?"

"If you would."

Edward nodded. "I'll take care of it right away."

Dickerson was plainly relieved. "Thank you, sir." The butler gathered the tray. "Would you like me to sit with the young lady while you get some sleep?" he said, glancing toward the bed.

The woman was still resting in the middle of the mattress, sprawled over the tangled covers as if she were a rag doll that had been tossed there.

"No, she's completely out of it."

Dickerson's brows rose. "Really?"

"Absolutely. I get the impression this woman hasn't slept in weeks. Watch this."

Edward took his spoon and banged it against the edge of the tray, causing a thudding clang to reverberate through the room.

The woman on the bed twitched, rooted her head more deeply into the pillow, then slipped into slumber again.

"How astonishing," Dickerson said.

"It is, isn't it? Every now and then, I test her to see if she's really sleeping. It helps pass the time."

"Sir!" Dickerson said, in patent disapproval.

"I don't see any other recourse, Dickerson. I can't have her waking and seeing me reading this book. Heaven only knows how she might react to such a sight."

"True."

Dickerson gazed at the woman for several more minutes. Edward caught the same indulgent expression the old butler often adopted when Edward's mother was in residence.

"Well, sir, if there's nothing else you need..."

"No, thank you, Dickerson."

The butler bowed and retreated from the room. Before Edward could forget his promise, he reached for the phone and dialed Captain Hobbs's extension. Evidently, the man was hard at work on the latest whodunit installment, because when the speakerphone engaged, Edward could hear the click of computer keys.

"Captain Hobbs, I hear that the new whodunit scripts are coming along well."

There was a moment of silence, then: "Thank you, sir. I suppose Dickerson informed you of the plot changes."

"Yes, he did."

"Now, sir, before you chastise me, I think you should know that I—"

"No need to explain, Hobbs," Edward said, interrupting him. "Dickerson is ecstatic about his role. Absolutely ecstatic."

Quiet thrummed on the other end of the line. Then Hobbs cleared his voice and offered in a slightly squeaky tone, "Really?"

"Really. By all means continue— Oh, and Hobbs, see if you can't arrange for Dickerson to die in a rather compromising situation. He's had something of a crush on Ethel for the past ten years."

"Oh?"

Edward could hear the man's creative juices beginning to flow. In his own mind's eye, Edward was envisioning the plump, caustic woman who had been the bane of Dickerson's existence for ages.

"Yes. I've often wondered if the two of them have ever indulged in an affair."

He thought he heard something drop on the other end.

"Dickerson and...*Ethel?*"

"Mmm."

"I'll get to work on the rewrites immediately."

"Good night, Hobbs."

"Good night, sir."

As he hung up the phone, Edward began to laugh in earnest. Poor Dickerson. The man would be in a state of shock after reading the new script, but Edward hadn't been able to resist a little mischief-making. Truth of the matter was, he didn't know if

Ethel and Dickerson had ever exchanged anything but double-edged household instructions. But Edward had always thought the two of them acted as if they'd been married for years.

Heaven only knew the two of them already argued like a couple about to share their golden wedding anniversary.

Boris lay upon the stretcher, his uniform soaked with blood, the sheet covering his hips gleaming with the crimson liquid. Finally, mere miles from the city's outskirts, his eyes flickered, and I bit my lower lip to keep from crying.

He was alive. Alive!

"We're almost there."

His brow furrowed.

"Where?"

The whisper was so piteously weak, my eyes stung from the effort to keep my tears at bay.

"I'm taking you to the hospital." I gripped his hand tightly, knowing that at any moment he might slip back into unconsciousness. Somehow, I felt that if I willed him to live, some of my strength might flow into his body and he would be whole again.

Closing my eyes, I envisioned him as he'd always been, a dashing sophisticate, a swashbuckling wooer of women, an incredible soldier, a man a woman would die to claim as her own...

"No wonder she mistook me for Boris," Edward mumbled to himself, tongue in cheek.

Dashing sophisticate, wooer of women and *incredible soldier* had never been terms linked to his own name. If not for the coloring he shared with Boris, Edward might have thought the woman truly "tetched."

Sunlight was streaming through the bedroom windows, and he knew he should hide the novel he'd been reading all night with the others, but he wanted to finish one more chapter.

He had only to walk into a room to make female hearts pound. The prowling grace of his gait was like that of a jungle animal in need of taming...

"Oh, yeah. He sounds like me," Edward muttered facetiously. "Suave, somewhat primitive, a draw to the ladies..."

And impotent.

Edward's consciousness screeched to a halt, and he reread the paragraph where Anushka was delicately explaining Boris's wounds to him.

Impotent?

This woman thinks I'm impotent?

He looked up from the pages to regard the woman on the bed with disbelief. He and the fictional character might share dark hair and blue eyes, but not being able to...

Damn it, was that why she continually freed herself from his embrace? Was she less tortured by conscience, as he'd believed, and more tortured by his inability to...you know?

Springing to his feet, Edward began to pace the length of the room. Even as a part of him insisted that he shouldn't take the confusion of an injured woman seriously, another part was both miffed and insulted. Every time he held Anushka in his arms, he'd struggled to remember the chivalrous creed his mother had imparted to him. He had done his best to cool his own raging arousal so that he wouldn't take advantage of the great Anushka, princess of espionage. And all the time she'd mistaken his manners for an old "war wound."

Hadn't she felt his arousal? Hadn't she sensed the way he trembled whenever she drew near? Hadn't she known that, emotionally, he was on the brink of...

Whoa. What was he thinking of here? That he was growing fond of this woman? This stranger? This...fruitcake?

But even as the inner railings were voiced, Edward stopped his pacing, planted his hands on his hips and regarded the woman tucked beneath his mother's blankets.

"I wondered when you would admit what was happening, sir."

Edward didn't move a muscle when Dickerson's voice slid out of the quiet.

"I don't know what you're talking about, Dickerson."

The old man smiled and set a tray of fruit, sweet-breads and coffee on the bedside table.

"Don't I, sir?"

"No."

When Dickerson straightened, his gaze was filled with silent reproof.

"I've known you since the day you were born—right there, on that bed."

Edward shifted. Would he ever grow so old that the household staff wouldn't remind him of such things?

Dickerson fussed with the lacy edge of a napkin, the position of a cup and saucer. Then he approached Edward, dolefully shaking his head.

"You were always a very lonely little boy."

"I—"

"And it wasn't because of the kidnapping," Dickerson said, overriding the response Edward had been about to make.

Circling his younger charge, Dickerson drew the rumpled tuxedo jacket from Edward's shoulders. Until that moment, Edward hadn't realized that he was still completely dressed from the previous evening's activities. He'd been so engrossed in Analee Adler's novels, he hadn't even bothered to change.

"You have an old soul, Master Babcock."

Again, Edward felt as if he were in short pants and was being readied to meet with his governess.

"I recognized the fact immediately," Dickerson continued, "because I suffer from the same malady." He began loosening Edward's cuff links.

"We old souls must stick together. Otherwise, our lives can become a very solitary business."

His hands deftly removed the last of the studs and slid the shirt from Edward's back. "See to your shoes and socks, sir. Then you can take a shower. I'll watch the princess for you until you return."

"She isn't a princess, Dickerson," Edward grumbled as he reluctantly complied with the butler's orders.

"Isn't she?"

Edward sat on a chair by the window, unlacing his shoes.

"Personally, I choose to think of her as being very royal indeed."

Edward sighed. "Anushka is a fictional character."

"I wasn't speaking of her identity, sir. I was referring to her ability to inspire love."

Edward dropped the second shoe on the floor and rested his elbows on his knees, suddenly weary.

"We don't know if she's inspired anything so lofty," he murmured, uncomfortable sharing his emotions with anyone, but sensing that Dickerson was probably the only person in whom he could confide.

"Don't we, sir?" Dickerson inquired, in a voice equally soft.

When Edward met the older man's gaze, he found a fond pride lingering in Dickerson's expression.

"I've only known her for...what? Forty-eight hours?"

"The heart has its own timetable."

"But it isn't rational to expect a person to—"

"Love is very rarely rational. In my opinion, love is very much like finding a kindred spirit. There are times when one meets a person and feels as if that person has always been a part of one's life. Love comes just as swiftly, just as surely. It's merely our ability to recognize its presence that delays the process."

"But I don't even know her real name."

"Does such information matter? Would your emotions change along with her title?"

Edward rubbed his hands over his face. "No, I suppose not." He squeezed his eyes shut and rubbed at the kinks in the back of his neck. A headache? No, just bone-tired weariness.

"Unfortunately, Dickerson, there is one stumbling block to this entire situation."

"What could that possibly be? The girl is perfect. She is sweet and kind and full of life. She laughs with as much passion as she lusts."

Edward abruptly stood, uncomfortable with that line of argument.

Dickerson continued, "You can't possibly think she is after your money, because she doesn't know who you are."

"It's not the money, Dickerson."

"Then what?"

Edward filled his lungs with air, then slowly exhaled. "I agree with everything you've said. I've had more fun since stumbling into this web of intrigue than I've had my whole life. This woman is maddening and awe-inspiring all at once."

"So what is the problem, sir?"

Edward moved toward the bed, his eyes tracing the sweet outline of the woman beneath the sheets. A woman known only as Princess Anushka. A person who didn't exist.

"I know all the wonderful things about her, Dickerson, but until I know her name—" he glanced up at his longtime manservant "—I don't know if she's free to love me."

Chapter Ten

Edward yawned, a part of his consciousness warning him that it was time for him to awaken. But his body and the rest of his psyche demanded more sleep. He was dead tired, and the settee he'd chosen to sleep upon was less than uncomfortable. He could feel one of the armrests lying beneath his neck like a rock, and the other was hooked beneath his knees in such a way that his feet dangled toward the floor. He'd raided pillows from some of the other chairs in the sitting room in an effort to keep his arms in line with his body, but a crick was developing in the small of his back. At that moment, he would have paid a thousand dollars for an hour on a king-size firm-support mattress.

Bam!

Edward jerked, the shreds of sleep scattering as a door slammed somewhere in the vicinity of his awkward resting place. Blearily he tried to focus.

"It's about time you awakened, Boris."

That voice. It conjured up the image of long legs, scanty underwear, a derringer hidden in the top of a woman's stocking, a dagger sheathed between her breasts.

His eyes fluttered shut again, and he smiled, more than willing to settle back and dream again.

But after a moment or two, he became distinctly aware of being watched. No. Not watched. Studied. Scrutinized. Evaluated.

Bit by bit, he opened one eye enough to see Princess Anushka standing nearby, her brows knit together, her toe beating an impatient tattoo on the carpet.

Daring to open the other eye, Edward peered up at the woman who stood next to the armoire, his body enduring a rush of adrenaline when he noted her pale blue teddy, garters and white silk hose.

"I didn't hear you get up," he grumbled, rubbing at his eyes and wondering if this woman was part of a dream from which he still hadn't awakened. A dream that had begun days ago, when he went diving. Perhaps he'd fallen asleep on the dock, and the whole improbable situation with this unknown woman had been nothing but fantasy.

"Obviously." Her eyes twinkled. "It's nearly eleven."

It wasn't a dream. This woman was real, very much alive, and ready to test the endurance of his wits yet again.

Edward dropped his head against the back of the settee. Nearly eleven, she'd said. His mind slowly absorbed the information. "Is that all?" He'd relieved Dickerson at ten, so that meant he'd been asleep about...

Twenty minutes.

"I planned on wearing the Vionnet today."

Edward didn't have the slightest idea what she was referring to. Was a Vionnet another of her wispy bits of lingerie? A daring sort of gown? A designer? Or a pair of eyeglasses?

"Well?" she prompted, when he didn't immediately reply.

Belatedly Edward realized that Boris had developed a habit of commenting on Princess Anushka's wardrobe. Indeed, the book continually drew attention to the fact that, for a man's, his taste in clothing was extraordinary. In fact, if Boris hadn't been afflicted that he couldn't...you know...well, he would have been the perfect companion for Anushka.

Anushka, on the other hand, had a keen appetite for sex, if the number of lovers in her books was anything to judge by. She was passionate, sensual, and infinitely intriguing. While Boris, on the other hand, was...

You know.

A slow irritation rose in Edward's chest. Was that what this woman thought of him? That he was like Boris in every way?

Every way?

His irritation quickly blossomed into pique, and then a full-blown anger.

No woman had ever complained about his attention before. Heaven only knew that he had kissed this particular woman on enough occasions, held her, caressed her, that it should be obvious that he wasn't...

You know.

"Boris, you're not paying attention."

Wrenched away from his thoughts, Edward frowned. This woman should know that she had only to walk into a room to bring him to a fever pitch of arousal.

She pouted at his evident inattention. "Should I wear the Vionnet or not?"

"Show me," he finally ordered, in what he hoped was a very Boris-like way. In fact, he was very pleased with the way he directed his own frustration into the character he played, knowing that he'd averted displaying his ignorance about whoever— or whatever—a Vionnet was.

Anushka withdrew a gown made of a whisper of silk organza pieced together from geometric shapes of sea green, azure, gray and white. Gossamer scarves fell from the short sleeves and, once again, Edward was struck by the authenticity of the clothes Princess Anushka had at her disposal. These were not the clever costumes most of the other guests were wearing. The workmanship and exquisite fabrics screamed of vintage haute couture.

"Where did you get that?" he asked, more for something to say than out of genuine curiosity.

"A little shop in Atlanta." She disappeared into the bathroom again.

It was several moments later when her answer finally wriggled its way into his brain.

Atlanta? According to the books he'd skimmed, Princess Anushka refused to set foot in the "heathen colonies." Was the mention of the southern city another clue to this woman's true identity?

Reaching for the phone, Edward punched the number for the security bungalow.

"Rafferty here."

"Any luck discovering the identity of our guest?" Edward asked without preamble.

"We've interviewed most of the invitees who didn't respond to our RSVPs. None of them had any idea who the woman could be. I still have three more people to find who indicated they would be coming, then didn't. I should have them tracked down within the next few hours."

"Good. I've also discovered that our guest bought the antique gown she's planning to wear today somewhere in Atlanta. It's a long shot, but since the gown is an original Vionnet, you might be able to find something along those lines."

"What's a Vionnet?"

"Not what. Who. Vionnet is an exclusive designer, so I'm sure such purchases are rare. If you could get a picture of the gown today and fax it to those antique stores that deal in haute couture, maybe we could get lucky."

"It's worth a try," Rafferty said. "Oh, and I also tried to get in touch with Analee Adler, just to see if she was aware of any wealthy fans who might cross paths with some of the folk on our original guest list. She's been in Rome for the past three weeks, on vacation, but is expected back at any time. Her housekeeper took my name and number and a description of our mystery guest.''

"Good idea.''

There was a long pause, then Rafferty inquired, "So...have you read the books?"

For some unaccountable reason, Edward felt heat seep up his neck. "Yes." He bit the word out. "Why?"

The security man chuckled, then said, "No reason. I'll touch base with you as soon as I—"

A mumbled conversation came from Rafferty's end, then the security man announced, "Doc Little wants to talk to you.''

A clattering followed the announcement, and then Doc Little's voice boomed across the line. "How is my patient this morning?"

"The same," Edward offered testily.

"Rats. I was hoping the sleep might coax her mind to relax its guard.''

"Well, it hasn't. Except for a reference to Atlanta, she still thinks she's Princess Anushka and that I'm her toady.''

Doc Little snickered.

"How was your reading?"

"You know damned well how my reading went. I discovered that this Russian bodyguard I'm supposed to be is impotent, damn it!"

Doc Little's laughter deepened to open guffaws.

"It isn't funny!"

"Sure it is. Just not to you."

"Well, I have half a mind to prove to the woman how mistaken she is," Edward offered, only partially joking.

Doc Little immediately sobered. "No! You can't do that. Remember, it is *vital* that the woman feel safe around you. You cannot, under any circumstances, do anything to make her think you aren't the man she believes you to be."

Edward opened his mouth to protest, remembering the evening in the study, when passion had raged between him and his princess and he'd nearly made love to her then and there. If another such clinch should occur, how could he possibly retain his control?

"Are you listening to me, Edward?"

"Yes." The word came through clenched teeth and was barely audible.

"Then you'd better take a long, cold shower and get that woman outside, so Rafferty can take a picture of her. We have a princess in need of her true identity, and you're the only man who can keep a lid on this risky venture."

"Great," Edward muttered to himself as he disconnected.

Raking his fingers through his hair, he willed himself to grow calm...calm...calm...

Damn, he thought...

No. Be calm. Calm and controlled.

"Boris, darling, who was on the phone?"

The sweet voice coming from the bathroom was nearly his undoing. Knowing that Anushka would be hot on the trail of some clue she thought she'd uncovered the night before, Edward forced himself to sit, then reach for his shoes. By the time he'd straightened again, he could hear Anushka humming in the bathroom.

"What are you planning to do today?" he asked, resting his forearms on his knees, since he was too tired to stand up.

When was the last time he'd pulled an all-night reading session? College? Graduate school?

"I take it that some formal activities have been planned for the guests?"

Edward thought for a moment, trying to remember the details of the gala. He'd left the preparations to Dickerson and the rest of the staff. He'd approved the overall scheme of events. But so far, he'd attended very few of the activities meant to impress the people he'd invited in hopes of coaxing them out of a million dollars or more. He'd been too occupied with Princess Anushka—a riddle unto herself.

"I think today's entertainments begin with a buffet on the terrace." Edward was sure that Captain Hobbs would use such a public gathering to further the plot of the whodunit. "Then there's a marathon of silent films in the library, dancing lessons in the gazebo, volleyball, croquet and tennis on the back lawn, and—"

The words jammed in his throat as Anushka

trailed out of the bathroom, wearing nothing but the lingerie she'd had on before.

"I thought you were planning to wear the... Vionnet," he said, hoping his voice didn't sound as gruff as he thought.

"I can't play tennis in chiffon, Boris. You should have thought of such a thing before you suggested it."

As far as Edward could remember, he'd suggested no such thing.

"What would you offer as a more sports-oriented choice?"

Damn it, what was he supposed to say? As was the case with most men, the only designers he was truly familiar with were Brooks Brothers and Mercedes-Benz.

Vainly he tried to remember one of the names he'd read in the novels from the night before. But the first book had been uninspired, and the second had involved Princess Anushka wearing nursing uniforms to allow her to work unnoticed at Boris's side.

"You...have so many to choose from," he finally said, hedging.

"Hmm," she said, and he hoped that meant she'd make her own decision.

She rummaged through the armoire again and held up a gown that appeared to be made of a finely knit wool. Even at a glance, Edward knew that the sweaterlike fabric would cling to every inch of Princess Anushka's frame.

"What about the Rochas?" she asked.

"Don't you think it will be somewhat hot?" he countered, knowing that for his own sanity, he would prefer she wear something looser. After all, he might be imitating the woman's Russian bodyguard, but that didn't mean he couldn't...

You know.

The doctor has already warned you about...you know...so don't even think about it. He was Boris. Boris the soldier. Boris the bodyguard. Boris the...

Wounded?

Damnation, it didn't matter if Boris had been wounded or not. His condition didn't make him any less a *real* man.

Pushing himself upright, he decided to have some real input in her decision. Unfortunately, when he got close enough to peek in the closet, he could smell the faint scents of lemon and rose on her skin, as well as the musky fragrance of perfumed talc.

"What about this one?" he suggested, retrieving a suit of striped tweed with fur at the cuffs and collars. The boxlike shape would disguise a good portion of her figure.

Anushka rolled her eyes. "Really, Boris. Wipe the sleep from your eyes. All that wool would be even hotter than the Rochas."

"Yes, of course."

He pointed to a sheath with a black skirt and a white-and-black geometric-print top. "How about that one?"

She sighed. "The Lelong is an afternoon costume."

"Isn't it afternoon yet?"

Pushing him aside, she withdrew a green gown with strips of satin that crisscrossed the hips. Below each strip was a ruffle of chiffon.

"Maybe it would be better if we avoided the sporting events altogether," she stated firmly. "After all, people are so much less likely to talk freely if they're hot and perspiring."

Edward didn't bother to reply. He was too busy ensuring that the gown she'd chosen would not prove detrimental to his health. Thankfully, he noted that the V neck was quite high, the sleeves were long and the last layer of ruffles would end at a point far below the knee. To many, the dress might even be considered matronly. It was something his mother would refer to as a "frock."

"What do you call that outfit?" he said without thinking, then could have bitten his tongue. He was supposed to be an expert on such things, after all.

But Anushka didn't seem to notice his gaffe. She patted him on the cheek, as if he'd made a particularly witty joke. "You know very well it's my Chanel 'Sitabout' dress."

She pointed to one of the drawers in the armoire. "I'll need to change lingerie."

Edward's attention zoomed back to her face to prevent his eyes wandering over the teddy she already wore.

"Whatever for?" he blurted.

She patted his cheek again. "Oh, Boris. You are a card."

Since that seemed to be the only answer he would receive, he willed himself not to watch her as she sashayed into the bathroom again.

"Bring me something else, Boris."

He hesitated, hoping she didn't mean what he thought she meant.

"I thought you wanted to wear the Chanel."

"I do, but I can't wear a blue teddy and white hose with a green dress."

Edward would have been more than happy to encourage her to do just that, but she was already saying, "Bring me something that matches and a pair of natural hose."

"Damn," he muttered under his breath.

Be calm. Be in control.

Realizing his palms were beginning to sweat as if he were a randy teenager about to escort his date to the prom, he swiped his hands down his trousers and opened the drawer Anushka had indicated.

Inside, he discovered mounds of frothy underthings in every color imaginable—apricot, yellow, white, pink, gold and black. There were tap pants and teddies, garters, waist cinchers and brassieres. If he hadn't known better, he would have thought he'd died and been sent to some male-oriented fantasyland.

"Boris?" Anushka called impatiently.

"Coming." His voice was nothing but a frog's croak.

Knowing he had to get this woman dressed—and wishing he wouldn't have such a vivid impression of what she was wearing beneath her gown—he quickly selected a mint green ensemble of what he remembered his mother once calling "scanties." The boxerlike panties, the bra and the wisp of a garter belt were extremely sexy, and he did his best to ignore the effect they had on his pulse as he grabbed a pair of hose and thrust the bundle through the bathroom door.

"Here."

The items were taken from him in a much more leisurely fashion than he would have wished.

"You could have brought them to me without holding them at arm's length."

"I...uh...thought I heard someone at the door."

Quickly shutting the princess in the bathroom, he strode to the outer door, opened it, closed it, then called, "Nope. False alarm."

There was some sort of muffled response from the bathroom, but he didn't try to decipher it. Instead, he raked his fingers through his hair and wondered why he was beginning to take leave of his senses.

Maybe that woman's problem is contagious.

He uttered a short bark of laughter, then looked down at his hands. They were trembling in a way they hadn't done since his first business merger.

For heaven's sake. He was a grown man. He'd had his share of romances. In college he'd even

been considered a campus catch—a title that had
been earned without anyone knowing his real name.

So why was he so flustered around Anushka?
Why did he feel like a kid who hadn't yet learned
where to safely put his hands? This woman was no
different from the scores of females he'd dated in
the past. He should be able to ignore whatever sensual instincts she inspired.

There had to be a logical reason for his bout of
inexplicable randiness. Perhaps he was acting so
oddly because he knew what sort of naughty wisps
of nothing she wore under her dresses.

But he'd had women appear at his apartment
wearing little more than a raincoat and a pair of high
heels before.

Then maybe it was her blatant sensuality.

Been there, done that.

Could it be the period clothes, or the way she
insisted on playing out this fantasy to the end?

No, if anything, that should have convinced him
to keep her at arm's length.

Then what?

At that moment, Anushka stepped through the
doorway wearing the green chiffon "Sitabout"
dress.

Edward swallowed to relieve the tension banding
his throat. The dress was by far the least matronly
"frock" he'd ever seen. The fabric clung to each
hill and valley of her body and fluttered ever so
slightly when she moved. The strips of matching
satin gleamed in the sunlight, drawing attention to

her hips and long legs. Last, and most intriguing of all, the ruffled bits of skirts hanging from the bands twitched when she moved, making him overly conscious of the way this woman walked, with the grace of Irene Castle and the sensuality of Marilyn Monroe.

Crossing to the armoire, she stepped into a pair of green satin shoes, tugged a rust-colored pair of gloves over her hands, then smoothed a green satin cloche with a rust ribbon over her hair.

"Well?" she asked, turning.

In an instant, Edward realized why this woman made him feel so charged, so alive. It wasn't because she was similar to the women he'd dated in the past. It was because none of the women he dated in the past had been *her*. What this woman thought of him mattered. It mattered more than anyone's opinion ever should.

And he certainly didn't want her to think he was incapable of making love to her.

"I think you're beautiful," he finally said, his voice low and filled with the wonder of his own epiphany.

His utter sincerity seemed to take her aback, then she smiled—somewhat shyly—and slid her arm around the crook of his elbow.

"Boris, would you be so kind as to escort me to brunch?"

"Yes, Anushka. I would be honored."

ANUSHKA carefully selected several different kinds of fruit, placing them in a colorful array on her plate.

She really was feeling quite rested today. There must be something to that adage about the sea air being good for what ails a person. She'd been a tad sluggish since her accident, and she vaguely remembered some unpleasantness the night before that had caused her to feel dizzy and weak. But after waking in her own bed, she'd reasoned that she must have imagined such symptoms.

Or maybe her uneasiness was all a dream. Heaven only knew why she kept thinking a water buffalo had somehow crossed her path and caused her to pass out from the sheer terror of the experience.

Shrugging away the silly idea, she turned her thoughts to more interesting matters. After such a complete night's sleep, she was eager to begin digging into the mystery of MEOW. As soon as she solved that particular mystery, she knew, she'd be able to finish that last chapter and wade her way through the galleys.

Her brow creased. *Galleys?* Whatever had caused her to invent such an odd word? Such fabrications were yet another sign of the way her exhaustion had taken hold of her faculties. Perhaps, after she'd gathered her clues, she should consider a nap.

Anushka was turning, a ripe red strawberry poised at her lips, when she noticed the butler marching through the garden. He'd barely stepped onto the stone flooring of the terrace when a large woman dressed in the black-and-white uniform of the household maids rushed toward him and threw her arms around his waist.

Hugging him as if he were a wrestler attempting to escape her grip, she cried, "Dickerson, please! You said you loved me! You said you adored me!"

Automatically Anushka looked to the butler for his reply. He licked his lips, offered a pained grimace and replied, "I *do*...love *you*, Ethel," he offered, with the oddest enunciation Anushka had ever heard from the man. In fact, if she hadn't known better, she would have thought he was reading from a script.

"Don't lie to me, Dickerson," the woman sobbed, clinging to him so tightly, his face began to redden from an obvious effort to breathe.

"I'm...not...lying!" With a supreme show of strength, the man managed to loosen the woman's hold. "I merely need time to—"

Before he could finish whatever he'd been about to say, a redheaded vixen dressed in a poor imitation of a Molyneux gown strolled onto the terrace and confronted Dickerson head-on.

"You said you loved *me*, you bastard," she hissed.

Anushka fought the urge to roll her eyes. She didn't approve of women who made scenes in public. In her opinion, excesses of emotion were always in poor taste—she'd told Analee as much on a dozen occasions. Moreover, any brazen hussy who didn't know that a tea gown was not to be worn

until after two in the afternoon obviously didn't
have the manners God gave a goose.

"Roxy," Dickerson protested, holding up his
hands.

Roxy? There was really a woman named Roxy?
That name made her sound as if she should be a
performer in some sort of penny opera—or worse
yet, a burlesque house.

"Damn you, Dickerson," she sobbed.

The guests gathered openmouthed around the
buffet table gasped as the redheaded woman
whipped a revolver from her pocketbook. A very
large revolver. Heaven only knew that with such a
weapon, she couldn't possibly have kept a compact
and a handkerchief inside, as well.

"Take this, you two-timing ne'er-do-well!"
Roxy screamed. Then, aiming down the barrel, she
pulled the trigger.

Chapter Eleven

Anushka's plate fell from her nerveless fingers. Without thought, she ran toward Dickerson—but not so quickly that the nefarious Dr. Little didn't reach the butler first.

"He's been shot in the chest!" Doc called. "I need a litter!"

Magically, a pair of burly men who looked more like gangsters than guests appeared with a stretcher. Before Anushka could even study the wound, they were carrying the butler away from the scene, leaving a trail of red droplets behind them.

Shocked, Anushka stood rooted to the ground, until Roxy dropped her gun and began to run away.

"After her!" Anushka called to the other guests.

Roxy disappeared behind a copse of sumac trees and daisies. A portly gentleman wearing a garish pin-striped suit, along with a skinny, bird-legged man in golfing knickers and her own elegantly attired Boris, gave chase.

Anushka meant to follow them, but the distraught

Ethel latched on to her like a burr that couldn't be shaken loose.

"No, no, no!" she wailed.

The woman was so pitiful that Anushka felt an immediate wave of empathy for her. But as time wore on, the woman's crying began to sound more like a whining siren, and Anushka had to restrain herself from slapping the maid to free herself from the grips of the woman's hysteria.

After some time, the portly man returned, beet-faced and empty-handed. Several minutes later, the guest with the fuchsia-and-green-plaid knickers made his appearance. Then, after nearly ten minutes, Boris came into view.

Viewing his arrival as a reprieve from her present hell, Anushka firmly handed Ethel to a woman sporting far too much makeup and skin so tightly stretched over her features that it didn't appear real.

She joined Boris, automatically searching him for some evidence of harm, but apart from the wind-blown rumpling of his hair, he appeared unscathed.

"Did you catch her?"

"No. She disappeared."

Anushka quickly scanned the crime scene, but in the fracas, the revolver had mysteriously disappeared.

"What on earth happened here, Boris?"

He shrugged. "A lovers' tiff."

She shook her head. "No. I sense that MEOW is involved."

Boris stared at her in disbelief. "You can't be serious. Nothing was stolen."

"Not yet," Anushka murmured, knowing by the slight twisting of her stomach that there was much more to the scenario than the quarrel they'd all witnessed. "I think that MEOW orchestrated this little scene to provide a diversion."

"For what?"

She met his gaze and held it.

"The robbery of the Czarina's jewels. They know we're here, Boris. What's more, they may know *why* we're here."

She straightened her shoulders like a veteran soldier. "Come on. It's time we got to work."

"SHE THINKS the whole scene was a diversion for MEOW," Edward said later as he sank into the chair behind his desk and gazed at the men who had joined him in the study.

Hobbs's mouth gaped. "But I followed your directions to the letter. I made it quite clear that Dickerson's 'death' was the result of a crime of passion."

From the wingbacked chair in a shadowy corner of the study, the "dead" man glowered at them both.

"The two of you planned this, didn't you?" he groused. "You meant for that Ethel woman to get ideas in her head. It's not bad enough that she's been pestering me for years."

Edward exchanged a quick glance with Hobbs,

then looked away when the man's eyes twinkled with mirth.

"We have no idea what you mean," Hobbs insisted.

"Oh, I'm sure that you do," Dickerson said ominously. "Due to this charade, I have become a—"

The door to the study opened, and Dickerson snapped his mouth shut. Retreating into the darkness, he appeared to be nothing more than a shadow.

Unfortunately, to the woman who brought a tea tray into the room, he was just the shadow she'd been looking for.

"Hello, Dickerson," Ethel drawled, her voice husky and intimate. "I brought you some…tea."

Seeing there was only one cup and saucer on the tray, Hobbs said, "Hey, what about—"

Before he could finish asking about their own refreshments, Edward grasped his arm and signaled for the man to remain silent.

Ethel set the tray on a nearby table, then grasped the napkin and positioned it over Dickerson's lap with a little more zeal than was necessary.

"You just call if you need anything else," she murmured throatily.

Edward managed to hold his mirth until Ethel closed the door. Then he and Hobbs dissolved into laughter.

Dickerson stood with utmost grace and threw the napkin on the tray.

"If that's how you mean to behave, I'll just leave

the two of you to your machinations," he said stiffly.

"Now wait, Dickerson," Edward said in an attempt to placate the man. "We need your help to disarm Princess Anushka's latest tangent."

The butler drew back his shoulders. "I believe that I would be of no help whatsoever. After all, as of eleven o'clock this morning, I am dead."

With that parting shot, he exited the room through a rolling bookcase.

Edward glanced at Hobbs again, and they both snickered. Pushing himself to his feet, Edward rounded the desk and stared at the glowing screen of the laptop computer Hobbs had brought with him.

"So what have you got planned for tomorrow, Hobbs?"

"I intended to have Roxy's body found at the bottom of a cliff, the victim of an apparent suicide."

Edward quickly read the description of the scene on the computer, then regarded the captain with raised brows. "You do realize that there is supposed to be a culprit to these crimes? Despite the fact that Anushka thinks we're involved in a very real plot, the rest of the guests are here to be entertained. They should have an opportunity to gather clues and solve the whodunit."

For an instant, Hobbs seemed taken aback. "Oh...well, of course I remember," he blustered. But it was obvious that he, too, had been drawn into the Anushka fantasy to the point where he was beginning to believe she really was the Princess.

Edward pinched the bridge of his nose. Everything was becoming so complicated. He had a nameless feeling that events were rollicking out of control, the pace building and building until they could only climax in disaster or...

Or a passionate evening with Anushka, a glowing fire and a bearskin rug.

No. He couldn't allow himself to think that way. He had to be Boris.

"I've got to get some sleep," Edward announced wearily. "I'll leave the script to you."

He was almost to the door when he turned to point at Hobbs and said, "Remember to keep the whole thing simple. Any more twists and turns in this mystery, and we'll have to call Scotland Yard to figure out an ending."

Hobbs's features fell in disappointment, but he finally shrugged and sighed. "Very well, sir."

Edward let himself out of the study, then nearly jumped when he saw Anushka leaning against the opposite wall, one knee crooked and her foot planted against the plaster. The inherently sensual posture, combined with a butter yellow evening gown edged with diagonal rows of beaded fringe, was enough to put a frustrated man over the brink. Only by a supreme effort of will did Edward manage to avoid rushing toward her, pinning her to the painted fresco and ravishing her.

Ravishing? Even his inner thoughts were beginning to adopt Boris's vocabulary. By the time this whole escapade was finished, it would be Edward who was carted away to the loony bin.

"What have you been doing?" Anushka inquired, her hands caressing the crystal fringe of her gown in a way that made the strands shimmer and dance.

"I was…er, interrogating Captain Hobbs."

She grimaced. "The careless one whose yachting skills landed me in the drink."

"Yes."

"I hope you scolded him."

"Quite soundly."

"But you didn't hurt him, did you?"

"Only a little."

Her smile was pure pleasure, and caused a heat to gather in Edward's loins.

Loins? Good hell, he was losing his mind, and his own manner of speech.

"Come with me, Boris."

She crooked her finger, and at that moment Edward knew he would follow her to the ends of the earth.

When she led him outside and began to walk to the cliff overlooking the landing, he asked, "Where are we going?"

"Somewhere we won't be overheard."

The night had grown black and still after an evening of charades and fine food. A slight sea breeze was the only real ripple in the calm—that and the fact that the woman beside him did not seem to be inclined to regain her sanity.

Sensing that the riffling air was cold on Anushka's shoulders, Edward shrugged out of his evening jacket and draped it over her shoulders. She sighed and smiled at him in gratitude, but there was something about that smile that held a tinge of sadness.

"Despite all that has happened here, Boris, I have truly enjoyed my stay on Babcock Island."

"Have you?"

"Mmm. There is something infinitely peaceful about this place."

"Many would call it isolated."

She shook her head. "Those who think so are obviously blind. The world is a chaotic enough place. A person needs somewhere to hide every now and then."

"You sound as if you were being chased like a fox at a hunt."

"In many ways, I often feel as if I am."

"Because you're a spy?"

She didn't answer, and he allowed her to sink into silence.

They reached the edge of the precipice, and Anushka seated herself on a large, flat rock, then indicated that Edward should do the same. For some time, neither of them spoke. Edward sat beside the woman who had the ability to make his body thrum with pleasure, frustration, disbelief and worry, and suddenly he couldn't imagine a life without her near.

Immediately he tried to banish such a thought. He'd only known this woman a few days—and he still didn't know her true self. He was infatuated with a fantasy.

But even as he tried to convince himself of the truth of the assertion, he found himself already dreading the moment Princess Anushka, queen of the spies, disappeared from his life.

Wordlessly he reached for her hand and wove their fingers together. He thought he saw her smile, but the darkness was growing more and more complete. Without a moon, he could not study her features. He could only feel her soul mingling in the darkness with his.

"Do you believe in fate, Anushka?" he asked after a very long time.

"I believe that there are things that happen in life that cannot be explained," she said after a moment of thought. "Good things come to us, happy accidents, and I often think an unseen force is responsible." He knew she turned to face him by the paler shadow of her skin and the rustle of her dress. "Like you, Boris. You have been one of the best things to ever happen to me."

He squeezed her hand, wanting to believe that when this masquerade was over, this woman would still feel the same way.

Unable to help himself, he leaned toward her, touching her lips with his own. Softly, reverently, he kissed her, imbuing the caress with all the nameless emotions this woman inspired in him. Then, knowing that he could not continue without taking the embrace to its logical and climactic conclusion, he pulled her close and tucked her head beneath his chin.

Tomorrow she would remember who she was, he reassured himself.

So why didn't the thought bring him any comfort?

"I THINK I've figured out what is going on here, Boris."

Edward listened with only half an ear as Anushka dressed—this time in the Vionnet that she had not worn the day before. He was absently finishing his toast while reading the third Princess Anushka novel, which he'd hidden inside a volume of poetry.

"Boris?"

He grunted to show he was listening, while in reality he was deeply involved in *The Spy Loves Twice*.

"I don't think that Dickerson was really killed."

A second passed before Anushka's statement penetrated his brain. Then Edward's head jerked up, and he gave the flesh-and-blood princess his undivided attention.

"Why would you say that?"

"The whole setup smells to high heaven. Why would Dickerson be the epitome of refinement one day, then a roving Romeo the next?"

"But we saw the woman shoot him."

"She could have used blanks."

"He was bleeding."

"Dickerson could have feigned a wound with honey and food coloring."

Corn syrup and food coloring, if the truth were known.

"But he had to be dead."

"None of us were able to examine the wounds. None but that scoundrel Dr. Little."

"But—"

"No, my mind is quite clear on this point, Boris. The murder was staged."

"But why?" he said weakly, knowing he had to contact Captain Hobbs immediately. Dropping his "poetry" onto the floor, he used his toe to slide the book beneath the cloth draped over the telephone table.

"Because MEOW knows we are here, and they want our investigation to be diverted by a wild-goose chase."

She emerged from the bathroom, her makeup flawless, her hair combed in sweeping waves, celluloid bangles at her wrist. As she lifted on tiptoe, Edward noted the seams of her stockings and wondered when society had deemed such things unfashionable. He, for one, liked the way the opaque strip drew attention to Anushka's long, delicate legs.

Even the dress she wore seemed to accentuate the delicacy of her calves and ankles. The white scalloped hem led to the pale blue of the skirt and torso, where geometric blocks of pale green and sage drew one's attention to her slim hips. At her elbow, long white scarves fell to her wrists, and another scalloped white band circled her neck.

When had women decided that such clothing was no longer fashionable, Edward wondered? Why had they ever been drawn to the staid suits of the forties, or the standoffish crinolines of the fifties, the absurdities of the sixties? In his opinion, fashion should return to the Roaring Twenties, when women had first begun to flaunt their sex appeal and wield their sensual powers over unsuspecting men.

As it happened, Edward would be more than happy to make an appeal to the world's fashion designers.

"Boris, would you, please?"

She indicated a white wide-brimmed hat on the top shelf of the armoire.

Standing, he moved close enough to retrieve the item she needed, then purposely lingered, brushing against her as he circled to face her. Softly, gently, he settled the hat over her silken hair, taking his time and managing to caress her cheek, her jaw, knowing all the while that he was playing with fire.

Boris wouldn't touch her this way.

He wouldn't have been able to bear reminding himself of the one thing he could never have.

"I like this one," he commented truthfully, enjoying the way the milliner had left most of the crown open to expose Anushka's hair. A pleated scarf wrapped around her forehead, then tied at her nape beneath the huge straw brim.

When he didn't move away, she grew inestimably

still. Edward knew from her posture alone that she was aware of him, aware of the proximity of his body, of his desire to touch her.

"We really should join the others," she murmured, her voice a wispy whisper.

"Why?" Unable to help himself, he cupped her shoulders, delighting in the way her warmth seeped through the gossamer fabric.

"We have a job to do," she said unsteadily.

"But I don't want to think about work. I don't want to think about anything but you."

Knowing he was playing with fire, he bent to brush a kiss against her neck.

"Honestly, Boris," she said, somewhat unsteadily. "I don't know what's come over you lately."

"And here I was sure you knew how you'd infected my blood," he rasped.

Drawing her into his arms, he kissed her, slowly, luxuriously, delighting in the taste of her, the shape, the texture. When he drew free, her eyes were wide with wonder.

"This isn't wise," she whispered.

"No. It isn't."

"We should put some space between us."

"Of course."

But neither of them moved. They were held in a silken spell of their own making, and even reality found it difficult to intrude.

In that instant, there was nothing on earth that Edward wanted more than to spend the day alone with her. He would have gladly given away his millions in exchange. And such deeply rooted need was more unsettling than he would have imagined.

"Why don't we go on a picnic?" Edward suggested, before he could examine his thoughts too closely. "Just the two of us. No one will even notice we're gone."

She hesitated, clearly torn between her duties and his tacit promises. Finally, she relented.

"Just let me get my pearls," she murmured.

Edward frowned. In all the time she'd been here, Anushka had never worn jewelry. Why would she feel the need to do so now?

Slipping out of his embrace, she moved to her dressing table. Stopped.

"What is it?" Edward asked when she stiffened.

"I—"

She began looking around the room, purposefully at first, then with growing agitation.

"Where is it?" she asked, her voice full of panic.

"What?"

"The Czarina's jewelry case."

Edward wasn't at all sure what she was talking about. She'd told him about the jewels, but he'd always thought that they—like everything else— were figments of her imagination.

"Perhaps it's in the armoire."

"No," she said, more desperately. "I would have seen it there."

Nevertheless, she ran to the closet and began searching its depths, throwing garments on the floor in her haste to find the item she sought.

"It isn't here!" she said, clearly panicking. "Someone has taken it, Boris."

"Now, Anushka—"

"No! Don't try to placate me! The case is gone!" Her skin grew pale and she swayed. "She'll kill me. She'll have my head mounted in her den."

"What?"

But Anushka wasn't listening to him. She ran toward him, grabbing fistfuls of his shirt in earnest supplication. "You have to help me. If the Czarina discovers I've lost her jewels—"

"I know, I know, she'll have your head mounted on her wall," he teased.

"No! Don't talk like that, don't make fun. The Czarina is a very powerful woman. Her temper is infamous. I will not escape punishment."

Edward began to realize that Anushka wasn't being overly dramatic in her supplication. Her skin was white, her body trembling. She was well and truly afraid.

"What does this case look like?"

She bit her lip in an effort to push her anxiety aside. "It—it's round, with a handle at the top. Hinges in the middle allow the case to open like a sliced melon to reveal the compartments inside."

"What color is it?"

"It—it's made of tortoiseshell, inlaid with gold and mother-of-pearl."

Try as he might, Edward couldn't remember seeing anything remotely like such a case, but he gripped Anushka's shoulders and said, "I know a man we can talk to. If the case is anywhere on the island, he'll know what to do.''

"Can he be trusted?" she whispered. "If MEOW is involved, we would be dragging your friend into certain peril."

"I trust him with my very life," Edward murmured, pulling her tightly against him and imbuing her with his own warmth. "We'll get to the bottom of this. I promise."

Chapter Twelve

Minutes later, Edward found himself leading Anushka to the security bungalow. At his arrival, Rafferty immediately rose from his desk, revealing a military background with his posture and purposeful expression.

"This area is restricted, sir. Ma'am."

After Anushka mentioned that she would be able to pinpoint Edward Babcock due to the deference given him by the servants, Edward had warned his men to be careful. Even so, he wasn't quite prepared for the steely glare Rafferty leveled in his direction.

"We're quite aware of that, but we need some help."

"Oh?"

Rafferty didn't look the least bit interested.

"Ms. Anushka is missing a piece of her luggage."

Rafferty's mien didn't alter. He didn't even blink.

"Now see here!" Anushka snapped, forcefully pulling the man's chin in her direction. "This isn't an instance to act like a Cossack with a hangover. Time is of the essence, and lives are at stake.''

Edward had to applaud Rafferty's nerves of steel. He didn't blink at such a pronouncement.

''Really, madam?''

''Yes! A case has been stolen. A very valuable case filled with jewels.''

''You have a description, I suppose?''

''Of course I have a description. The case was put into my care by the Czarina herself.''

Rafferty's expression shifted ever so slightly. ''Ah. I think I know which one you mean. It is small, round, made of gold and—''

''Yes, yes! That's the one.''

''I believe it is still in the harbor.''

Anushka blinked, her dark eyes becoming even more inscrutable.

''I beg your pardon?''

''The case is in the harbor, somewhere on the sea floor.''

She glared at him as if he were personally responsible.

''Whatever for?''

''I believe that you were holding the case when your…unfortunate accident took place. I had a report from several witnesses that you were clutching the case mere minutes before the boat docked. When the case fell overboard, you attempted to retrieve it.''

Edward waited for a snappy comeback from the

princess, but none came. Instead, she weaved slightly, as if about to...

"Catch her!" Rafferty cried, just as Anushka's knees buckled, and Edward scooped her into his arms.

Rafferty opened the door to the infirmary, but Edward shook his head. "Due to the way she's grown suspicious of Doc, I think we'd best take her somewhere else."

Rafferty took a set of keys from his desk and opened a small room to the right of his office. The windowless cubicle held a bed, a dresser and another door, leading to a minuscule bathroom. Besides being used as a resting spot for security men during late hours, the area had become an impromptu holding cell for nosy reporters and pesky paparazzi who tried to sneak onto the island.

Setting Anushka on the mattress, Edward reached for the blanket folded at the foot of the bed, but she was already beginning to stir.

Edward motioned for Rafferty to wait in the other room.

Without warning, Anushka sat bolt upright and grasped both of Edward's hands.

"Meow."

He stared at her, taken aback, then realized she was referring to the infamous ring of thieves that she believed were on the island.

"What about them?"

"They are responsible for the case's predicament."

"But Rafferty said—"

"I know what he said, but the fact remains that I would not allow the Czarina's jewels to be lost—for any reason. Therefore, they must have arranged for my...'accident.'"

"But—"

She clasped his hands again, holding them against the warmth of her bosom, and for a moment it didn't matter that this woman was delusional. All that mattered was the warmth of her body, the sweet curves of her breasts, the supplication of her grip.

"We have to do something quick. MEOW might know the location of the jewelry case—they may even have already retrieved it. We must find out, one way or the other."

Edward was finding it difficult to think at all, let alone to plot against an imaginary ring of jewelry thieves. Anushka's eyes had grown wider, larger, darker. Her supplication tugged at his very soul, and he found himself wondering how he'd managed to resist her feminine allure thus far.

But then again, he hadn't resisted her. Not quite. Not entirely.

His gaze fell to her lips and, unable to help himself, he bent, covering her mouth with his own, hungrily searching the sweet warmth of her, the taste of her, the enchantment of her. Unconsciously, his hands moved around her back and drew her to him—so close that he didn't note the way she rose to her knees or the way he bent precariously to meet her halfway.

When his lungs screamed for air, he drew away, but not far. He was still so close he could feel the silken caress of her skin, the puff of her own breath against his cheek.

"Boris?" Her voice was so soft, so husky, so vulnerable, he knew immediately what she meant by the query.

"I can't help it. I can't stay away from you. The minute you look at me, I feel as if I'm falling into your gaze. I feel as if I've known you for years and years."

Not until the words had been said aloud did Edward realize how true they were. He knew nothing about this woman—her background, her family, her education, her identity. All were mysteries to him. After so many years of avoiding anyone who could uncover his true identity, Edward had grown wary of women who appeared to have secrets.

Yet here he was, confronted with a situation he couldn't explain and a woman he couldn't ignore...and he didn't care. Something about her, something about her innate goodness, caused him to trust her in the same way he trusted Rafferty, Doc Little, Dickerson and Captain Hobbs.

But there was so much more to his emotions than that.

Anushka framed his cheeks with her small, soft hands. "Don't do this, Boris. We can't torture ourselves with things that can never be."

"Damn it, Anush—"

She stopped his protestations by laying her fingers over his lips.

"No. We could never be happy together. Not in the way you mean."

"Why?"

The moment the word burst from his mouth, Edward realized just how far his involvement with this woman had gone. He was actually considering a relationship. An honest relationship. One that included the confession of his own identity and his own longing for companionship.

"We both have different needs," Anushka whispered, jarring him from his thoughts.

"How can you say that? I can feel the way you tremble in my arms."

"Yes, but I require more." Her eyes grew sad. "Please, Boris. Let's leave our discussion there."

He shook his head. "No. Tell me what you mean. Tell me where I fall short in your estimation."

Her expression grew pained. "I need...sex, Boris."

Boris couldn't make love.

But wasn't lovemaking more than a mingling of bodies? Wasn't it also a melding of minds and spirits?

Unable to control the passion that raged through his senses, he promised himself, *Just one kiss, one caress.*

Then she was in his arms, and he covered her mouth with his own. Slowly, he lowered her to the bed, his weight pressing into her. Again and again, his lips slanted over hers, until they were both breathless and his body felt on the verge of spontaneous combustion. Seeking some small measure of control, he kissed her cheek, her neck, the hollow between her collarbones.

"Is this what you want?" he whispered, needing her reassurance that he was free to continue.

Without warning, she pushed at his chest, causing him to tumble onto the floor. Then, before he could stand, she ran from the room.

Distantly he heard the slam of the main door. Mere seconds later, Rafferty appeared in the threshold, a grin tugging at his lips.

"I thought you told me you'd read the Princess Anushka books."

Edward groaned.

He *had* read them. But Boris was supposed to be impotent, not dead.

Groaning to himself, he pressed the palms of his hands against his aching eyes. Lack of sleep and Anushka's appearance in her underwear this morning had completely muddled his thinking. He was supposed to make this woman safe, damn it. He was supposed to treat her with all the chivalry of a knight.

Instead, he'd forced her to voice her desires, then proceeded to make love to her anyway.

Belatedly he realized that he'd unconsciously yearned for this woman to recognize him as who he was, instead of a character in a book.

His hands dropped, and an overwhelming sense

of defeat swept through his body. What was wrong with him? He wasn't some toad who repelled the fairer sex. Yet this woman didn't love *him*, she wasn't attracted to *him*, she wasn't even kissing *him*. She was involved with Boris, drawn to Boris, communicating with Boris—a man she believed she'd known for years. In allowing himself to forget such a fact, Edward had unwittingly fallen in love with a mirage.

His mind screeched to a halt, latching on to a single word.

Love?

He wasn't in love. He couldn't possibly be in love. He'd only known this woman for a few days, and in that time, she'd managed to throw his life into total chaos. He, too, was drawn to an image, not to reality. If he actually knew this stranger's identity, he probably wouldn't love her at all.

He was sure he wouldn't love her.

Wasn't he?

"Do you need some help off the floor?" Rafferty asked dryly.

"No. But thanks anyway."

Rolling to his feet, Edward made a show of dusting himself off, even though the security bungalow was kept in pristine order.

"Any luck in finding out who she is?" Edward asked in what he hoped was a casual voice.

"Nothing definitive, but we've got a few leads. One of the women who received an invitation passed it on to a sorority sister to use. Evidently she wasn't aware of your policy of refusing all gate-crashers. I'm still trying to track down the sorority sister."

"Good. The minute you know anything, let me know."

"Sure."

Gathering as much of his dignity as he possibly could, Edward exited the security building, then paused, breathing deeply of the crisp, salty air.

He didn't love this woman. Not at all. He was merely caught up in the fantasy of her choice of identities. As long as he remembered such a fact, he would be able to keep his thoughts and emotions—and urges—in line.

He was sure of that.

Quite sure.

Wasn't he?

ANUSHKA RUSHED down the steps leading from the cliff to the landing below. She didn't really know where she was going or why. Her entire being was focused on the glorious sensations thrumming through her veins, as well as the impossibility of the entire situation.

To allow Boris to touch her in such a manner was madness, sheer madness. Such a dalliance in sensual pleasures could only hurt them both. That was why Boris had insisted they not make love before he went to war. He'd told her that he wanted to wait until their wedding day. He'd wanted their wedding night to be special, traditional, wonderful.

She knew now that he'd been lying to her all along. He hadn't wanted to make love with her at all. He'd merely wanted to clean out her bank account and leave her penniless. Boris had...

Her brow creased in confusion, and she stumbled on the staircase. Her legs began to tremble unmercifully, and she sank onto one of the granite blocks. Her temples throbbed with weariness and an unbearable tension. Boris was to blame. Boris had betrayed her. Boris had...

No, not Boris. Boris had always been kind and loving and wonderful. Some other man...

A face swam in front of her mind's eye. A devilishly handsome face with sun-streaked hair and brilliant green eyes. A surfer's body...

His name... What was his name...?

Graham?

No.

Gray?

Greg.

Greg. Greg Chaney.

She scrunched her eyelids tightly together, as if the action would help her to see the image more clearly.

Funny, but she was sure that the mere mention of him used to cause her blood to boil. But today she couldn't seem to summon any emotion stronger than annoyance.

Had she really been tempted to make love to such a self-absorbed, egotistical pretty boy? Her head ached from the abominable effort it took to think, but she couldn't imagine anything about the man that had ever charmed her.

What was the matter with her? Since the accident, she'd had a horrible time remembering things. The past still seemed so muddled.

Maybe she was sick. Maybe she had injured herself more than she had supposed. Such an explanation would certainly make sense of this Greg person her mind insisted she'd once loved.

No. It wasn't possible. She would never be so desperate for company that she would choose such a milksop over Boris.

Boris.

The hairs at the back of her neck tingled, and her nerves became alert and overtly conscious of her surroundings. The roar of the sea filled her ears, the squawk of the gulls. The sun beat unmercifully on the top of her head. Even so, gooseflesh pebbled her arms and her heart flip-flopped in something akin to joy.

Without looking, she knew that Boris had stopped on the stair above her and now towered over her like some ancient tree, completely formidable, yet somehow safe and reassuring.

"You aren't feeling well." The words emerged from his lips as a statement.

"I'm fine," she insisted breezily, but even to her own ears, she sounded weary and frazzled.

"No. You're not."

He sat next to her on the warm step, the length of his thigh crowding hers.

"Tell me what you're thinking," he urged.

She was tempted to confide her confusion, but resisted the luxury. How could she possibly explain that the thoughts and images rushing through her brain made no sense whatsoever? The memories were so foreign, they seemed to be those of another person.

Another person...

Another person?

Preposterous.

Stiffening her spine, she forced herself to recall how she'd come to be on this rock overlooking the ocean.

MEOW.

The Czarina's jewels.

How could she have been so stupid as to let her own petty concerns block out the one overwhelming problem that faced her?

Panicked, she blurted, "We've got to find that case. We have to determine if MEOW already has possession of it."

The man beside her remained silent for several minutes and she prayed he would allow the change in subject. She didn't feel up to speaking about herself anymore. There were so many things to do. The golden jewelry case had to be located, the next manuscript finished, galleys proofed...

"Since we don't know who the members of MEOW are," Boris commented, "I think we'd best check on the case first."

"How?" she said quickly, forcing her thoughts back into line.

"We'll have to take a look underwater." He pointed to the wooden dock. "There's a strong current close to the shore there. I would imagine such a case would be picked up and carried out to sea."

Her fingers grew cold at the mere thought.

"No. It has to be there. It can't have been swept away." She turned to Boris, instinctively gripping his arm. "Please! You have to help me."

He covered her hand with his own, his eyes filling with a tenderness she couldn't believe was directed to her.

"Of course I'll help you. I just want you to be realistic about the possible outcome. If the case has been taken too far out to sea, there's no way we'll find it."

She nodded to show she understood. But being forewarned of such a catastrophe did not make it easier to bear.

"How can we find out what has happened down there?"

He squeezed her fingers. "Leave that to me. Go on up to the house and get into your bathing suit. Meet me on the pier in fifteen minutes."

For some reason, she felt a sharp twist of fear. "B-bathing suit?"

"Yes. You'll have to get into the water, and I don't think that dress is very practical for such an activity, do you?"

"I—I could stay on the landing and..."

"I need you with me to help look. You've given me a good description of the case, but that doesn't mean I could find it as easily as you could."

Anushka didn't know why the thought of entering the water terrified her so completely. After all, she'd once tried to swim the English Channel, and she'd spent most of her summers vacationing near the Black Sea.

Shaking away her impressions of impending doom, she rose to her feet and hurried back to Babcock Mansion. A part of her resisted each step she took, but another, more insistent part worried that Boris might change his mind and refuse to look for the missing jewelry if she didn't hurry.

Automatically she used the secret entrance Boris had shown her. Once in her rooms, she flung the armoire door wide.

Had she even brought a bathing suit? She couldn't remember. Examining the hangers filled with clothing, she sighed in something akin to disappointment when she located a Worth cover-up made of the finest navy wool. It was styled much like a cape, but a tiny appliqué of a mermaid prevented any ideas of mistaking the garment for anything but what it was.

That meant that she must have a bathing costume somewhere.

Digging through the drawers, she managed to locate a pair of canvas swimming slippers, complete with long twill ribbons to lace around her ankles. After a few minutes more of searching, she located a scoop-neck, thigh-length one-piece wool bathing suit, and another, scantier maillot of black Lycra.

Frowning, she wondered briefly if she was ill. For some reason, her mind refused to cooperate this morning. She kept thinking she'd never worn these garments before, yet they were hers. She was sure of it.

Deciding that common sense was often the best course, she stripped and stepped into the maillot, then the wool bathing costume, the slippers, and finally the cover-up. Grabbing a beretlike beach hat and two towels from the bathroom, she ran back to the cliff and the steep stone steps.

Boris was already waiting for her, in a gleaming teak launch. He wore some sort of odd garment made of a fabric similar to rubber.

"You look like a frog," she called gaily as she made her way to the dock.

Boris's smile was wry. "That's what you said when I pulled you out of the drink a few days ago."

She stepped onto the pier, then hesitated. "I suppose that you intend to have me get in that boat."

"It would make matters a good deal easier."

"I thought I fell close to the pier."

"Yes, but the current goes out to sea. The force is strong for a hundred yards through a submerged reef, then becomes fairly calm again. I thought we might be better off starting farther out and working our way back."

The plan sounded perfectly logical, but her heart had begun to thud in her breast.

"I get seasick."

"Princess Anushka? Seasick?" he countered. "You must have yourself confused with someone else."

For some reason, his gaze seemed peculiarly intense, the blue of his eyes so vibrant and alive it rivaled the ocean behind him.

"Besides," he added, "we'll only be in the boat for a few minutes."

Seeing no other alternative in the situation, Anushka allowed him to take her hand and help her into the boat. Once she was there, the hot sun soaked into her navy cover-up until the fabric grew unbearable.

Since they would be in the water within a few minutes, she dropped the cover-up on one of the seats, then stiffened when she heard a snicker from Boris's direction.

"Is something wrong?" she inquired haughtily.

"Not at all." But his eyes betrayed him. They sparkled with overt humor as he scanned her from head to toe. "Are you afraid of a sunburn or something?"

"Why do you ask?"

He opened his mouth to offer a rejoinder, then obviously changed his mind. "No reason." He untied the launch from its moorings and pointed to her canvas shoes. "I think you can get rid of those."

"Whatever for?"

He jumped into the boat, causing it to rock. Immediately she felt her stomach lurch. "I don't think they'll fit inside your flippers."

"Flippers?"

He must not have heard her, because he gunned the engine, and the boat veered away from the landing.

She grabbed for the side of the boat. Then, seeing the water race past, she sank into a seat and purposefully fixed her gaze on Boris.

"Have you done any diving?" he shouted over the noise of the motor.

"No!"

"Then this will be an adventure for you!"

Anushka wasn't sure whether she wished to participate in such an adventure, so she didn't offer a reply.

In no time at all, they had closed the distance between the shore and the slight color change in the water that Boris had informed her was due to the reef's abrupt end.

Cutting the engines, Boris allowed the boat to coast to a stop, then pushed a button so that a brass anchor dropped over the side and held them in place.

Abandoning his role as captain, Boris pulled a tarp free from the equipment he'd stacked on the floor. Anushka sucked in her breath when she saw the diving paraphernalia—masks, flippers, tanks...

"I really don't think it's wise for me to accompany you," she said, her heart pounding, her sense of doom increasing.

"I'm not proposing that you delve twenty miles below the surface. The water here is little more than thirty feet deep. I'll give you a crash course in diving, then have you hover above me while I search the floor. That way, if I find something, I can check with you before proceeding."

"Why would you need to check with me? You know what the case looks like."

"But we don't have any guarantees that the case remained shut," he reminded her gently.

Anushka hadn't considered that particular point. If the case had burst open, the Czarina's jewels could be scattered far and wide.

"What do I need to do?" she said resolutely, refusing to surrender to her own nameless misgivings. She was, after all, a princess.

And Princess Anushka didn't know the meaning of fear.

Chapter Thirteen

Boris spent nearly an hour tutoring her, first in the boat as he introduced the various components, then in the water when he led her through the diving procedures. Finally, with her mask firmly planted over her eyes and the regulator clamped between her teeth, she held Boris's hand as he began a slow decent toward the ocean floor.

In no way was she prepared for the world that greeted her. She had always assumed that the water off the East Coast was cloudy and murky. But here, this far from the mainland, visibility was good and she could see for yards in directions. The azure sea was faceted by the broken shards of sunlight on the surface, and the irregular swatches of sunshine illuminated a patchwork of color from the reef, the vegetation below and the countless varieties of fish and other sea creatures inhabiting this part of the world.

Wordlessly Boris caught her attention and appeared to be asking if she was comfortable with her adventure so far. She nodded vigorously, then indicated that she would like to go even farther. For the first time, she felt in control near water. The breathing apparatus gave her a sense of security and safety, and she wanted to see more of this mysterious world.

Slowly, they swam down to the sea floor, leaving a cloud of velvety silt in their wake. She modified the way she kicked her feet in order to avoid clouding the water as much as possible, then eagerly watched as Boris took a flashlight from his belt and began to sweep the beam in front of them.

The light had dimmed so gradually, Anushka had not realized how many details had been hidden from her gaze. The roving shaft of gold illuminated even more tiny fish and gloriously colored vegetation, as well as rusted bits of metal and crustacean-covered shapes. Boris had told her before the dive that the reef had been responsible for more than one sinking, and here she saw the evidence of his assertion.

For the first time, she felt a rush of disappointment. When she envisioned searching for the Czarina's jewelry case, her mind had fabricated an image of a sandy beach covered with sparkling water. She hadn't considered how cluttered the area would be. How could she ever hope to find a small case the size of a melon?

With a flick of his wrist, Edward indicated that she should follow him in a crisscross pattern in front of the reef's opening. He had already warned her that, due to this being her first dive, they would remain submerged for only thirty minutes. Then, if need be, he would return as often as he could, until he thought the search was fruitless.

Time seemed to rush against her with the current. Vainly she strained her eyes to see through the muck and debris below her. At any moment, she knew, Boris would be signaling for her to go to the surface.

Dash it all, the case had to be nearby. It had to be!

She saw Boris begin to turn to face her and, automatically, she turned away from him so that she could ignore his signal for as long as possible. It was then that she saw a rounded shape partially hidden by vegetation.

Motioning to Boris, she quickly swam to the object, her heart thudding in her ears. As soon as she was close enough, she tugged at the weeds, revealing that a leather strap had caught around the branches. Filled with excitement and relief, she pulled at the case, freeing it from the green tendrils.

A layer of silt slid from the object, revealing the dull gleam of gold, the rich tortoiseshell and the iridescent mother-of-pearl. After a quick examination, she found, to her immense relief, that the clasp was still firmly in place. The case was completely intact.

She pointed to the surface, and Boris nodded. Slowly, patiently, they made their way upward until they popped out of the water. Gesturing toward the boat a few yards away, Boris swam toward the launch with great distance-eating strokes.

Anushka followed more slowly. She was suddenly conscious of a bone-tired weariness in her limbs, as well as a thudding tension in her head. She was working too hard lately, she realized. Much too hard. Her deadlines had come one on top of the other, and she knew she should take a vacation, but...

"Are you coming?"

She waved an arm to Boris, who had already hefted himself into the launch.

Handing him the case, she gratefully took the hand he extended to her and allowed him to pull her on board. He quickly began to unhook her equipment and strip her of the cumbersome gear, until she wore nothing but her woolen bathing suit. Glancing down, she realized the water had caused the tightly woven knit to cling to her body. Worse yet, it itched like the dickens.

Deciding that this was a time for comfort rather than fashion, she pulled the straps off her shoulders and stepped out of the suit, exposing the black maillot beneath.

When she looked up, Boris was staring at her hungrily, his eyes scanning her form.

"It's a good thing I didn't know you had that on before we went down," he said gruffly.

"Why?" She took a towel from one of the seats and rubbed it over her hair.

"We never would have made it as far as the water."

The electric tension she was beginning to expect

in his presence filled her body and crackled through her veins. She couldn't have moved if she tried.

"What's come over you lately, Boris?" she whispered. "Since we arrived, you've been so... intimate."

"Can you blame me?" He stroked her jaw with a finger that was still wet from their dive. "You've bewitched me through and through. I don't think I could ever let you go."

"But I'm not going anywhere, Boris."

His eyes grew sad, and she trembled, wondering what he wasn't telling her.

"I have grown to care for you," he whispered. "More than you will ever know."

She stared at him in amazement, feeling a rush of sensations—relief, confusion, desire, and a reciprocating adoration. Of course, she'd known of Boris's affection, but he had never voiced such thoughts before.

"And I care for you, too, Boris. Very much."

He seemed to hold his breath.

"Are you sure?" he asked after a moment's pause.

She nodded, the wealth of meaning behind her proclamation seeping into her brain. She had sworn that she would never give her heart to another man—and for years, she'd lived by that creed. Until now. In an instant, she knew she could never be whole unless she lived her life by his side.

"Yes." She wrapped her arms around his neck and held him close. "Yes, I'm sure. I will never leave you—no matter what challenges lie ahead of us, no matter what the future might bring.''

Then his lips were taking hers in a kiss that transcended mere desire. Even if he had not voiced his feelings for her, she would have known he adored her. He cherished her with his hands, worshiped her with his body. And when he drew away, she didn't feel cheated. Not in the least. It didn't matter that he couldn't...

''There are some things I need to tell you,'' he began, but she stopped him with her fingertips.

She shook her head. ''Not here. Not where anyone could find us and interrupt.'' She shivered, glancing up as a cloud drifted over the low-hanging sun and a chill crept over her skin. ''Let's go back to the house first. We'll make an appearance at dinner, then spend the rest of the evening in our room. Just the two of us.''

His lips spread in a smile that warmed her from within. ''I'd like that.''

He paused a moment to indicate the case at their feet. ''What about that? Don't you want to open it?''

She shrugged. ''The lock is fastened, so the contents are safe—if a trifle waterlogged. We can examine it later, once the water has been allowed to drain completely. That way, some of the smaller pieces won't accidentally float away.''

Boris flicked a finger beneath her chin. ''You're a very bright woman.''

This time, it was her turn to smile. ''Of course I

am. Otherwise, I would never have seen beyond your gruff and grumbly facade to the real man underneath.''

EDWARD REVELED in Anushka's laughter as she slung the ball-like case over her shoulder and ran toward the house.

"Last one in the bathroom will have to smell like a rotten fish,'' she called. Then she dodged through the door to the tunnel leading up to the east wing.

"Could I speak to you for a moment, sir?"

The voice eased out of the gathering shadows, and Edward froze, recognizing Rafferty's low tones. Automatically he halted in his tracks, watching Anushka disappear, then waited for the door to thump shut.

In those brief moments of quiet, his mind reeled. Was his idyll about to end? Was Rafferty here to tell him that the woman he'd pledged his soul to was a reporter? Or, worse yet, somebody's wife?

Steeling himself, he forced his expression to reveal none of his feelings. "What is it, Rafferty?''

The security specialist stepped from the puddle of darkness next to the trees. He looked grave—far too grave to be the bearer of good news.

"I have an update on the information you requested.''

Edward was sure that his heart offered a very real twinge of distress.

"Go on.''

Rafferty slipped his hand into his pocket and withdrew a small leather-bound notebook.

"I took your advice and faxed the picture of the Vionnet to some of the most exclusive antique shops in Atlanta. Two hours ago, I had a reply. I took the information I gained there and cross-checked it with a Ms. Sissy Munchausen—the woman who received Bunny Wilkerson's invitation."

"Wilkerson? As in Daniel and B. B. Wilkerson? The shipping magnate?"

"Yes, sir."

Edward's palm began to sweat, and he resisted the urge to wipe the clamminess away.

"Go on."

"The woman at Legacy Antiques remembered quite specifically who bought the Vionnet. The purchase was made by phone after Legacy Antiques put a Website on the Internet, advertising their most exclusive gowns. When the clerk took the purchaser's information, she chatted with the young woman and discovered she was a personal secretary for a novelist."

Edward's body grew cold.

"That novelist was Analee Adler."

A hand seemed to close around Edward's heart.

"I then spoke with Sissy Munchausen and sent her a fax of the same picture. She confirmed that she gave the invitation for the gala to Analee Adler, but that since Analee had been delayed in Rome, she had instructed her secretary to take her luggage

to Babcock Island and smooth over any unpleasantness with the security staff. Apparently Analee
was certain that Edward Babcock would welcome
her to the party with open arms, considering her
reputation with Babcock Publishing.''

The man grimaced, as if to say that Analee Adler
was very naive about the security arrangements at
Babcock Island during such a party.

''Ms. Munchausen also faxed me this. She told
me to offer her sincerest regards.'' His mouth
twisted again as he reached into his jacket, removing a grainy black-and-white article from the *New
York Times*. The caption read Novelist Greets Her
Adoring Fans, and the text briefly described an
autograph session at a bookstore in Manhattan. But
what caught and held Edward's attention was not
the article itself, but a face in the background that
Rafferty had circled with red ink. Despite the poor
quality of the copy, there was no denying the woman's delicate bone structure and glossy hair.

''The female I've circled is Ms. Carrie Randall,
Ms. Analee Adler's personal secretary.''

Edward took a deep breath. He had a name now,
a real name. Carrie Randall.

*Even so, would he ever stop thinking of her as
Princess Anushka?*

''What else do you have?'' he prodded, knowing
there was more.

Rafferty's smile was wry. ''What makes you
think I have anything else?''

''Because if you waited two hours to break this

news to me, you obviously spent the intervening time doing a complete background check.''

Rafferty chuckled. ''And here I thought I was a man of mystery.'' He rifled through his notebook again, then began to say, ''Carrie Randall is Caucasian, dark hair, dark eyes—''

''We *know* that much.''

Rafferty shrugged and mumbled to himself as he skipped lines. ''She has no priors...no misdemeanors, felonies—''

''Rafferty,'' Edward growled in warning.

''This is stuff you should know, sir,'' Rafferty said, tongue-in-cheek. ''Especially if you two decide to...go steady, so to speak, once she recovers.''

Edward didn't bother to demand how the man knew that Edward was considering such a move. No doubt, in the past few days, his employees had seen a side of him that they'd never seen before—that of a lovesick fool.

''Get on with it.''

''She's had one parking ticket—which she challenged, and received a reduced fine.''

''Smart girl.''

''She is the only daughter of Martha and Tom Randall, who live on Long Island. She graduated with honors from Saint Olaf's School for Girls, then obtained degrees in English and history from George Washington University.''

''Impressive.''

''For a short time, she was engaged to a...Greg Chaney, also of Long Island.''

Edward's fingers curled as an unaccountable wave of jealousy raced through his system.

"Mr. Chaney, on the other hand, has a rap sheet as long as both our arms put together—fraud, attempted fraud, larceny, grand theft auto. Evidently, Chaney charmed Carrie, convinced her of his undying love, then cleaned out her bank account."

"How did you find out all this?"

"A few computer checks and a chat with her mother. For the first time in my life, I didn't have to beg for someone to give me information. In fact, I nearly had to beg Mrs. Randall to stop. The minute she discovered I was doing a security check for the great Edward Babcock, she let loose with a flurry of interesting tidbits about our girl."

"Like what?"

"Her favorite color is blue, she's allergic to mosquitoes, she loves chocolate, Winnie the Pooh stuffed animals, sapphires and antiques—especially clothing."

Edward's brows raised. "Really?"

"Apparently her grandmother was a diplomat's wife during the Roaring Twenties. When the old gal died, Carrie inherited a good portion of the woman's estate and her extensive wardrobe. She's been collecting other pieces of vintage haute couture for years. Mrs. Randall said she only mentioned that fact because Carrie had been very reluctant to loan Analee Adler some of her items for the party, and would I please make sure Analee didn't spill anything during dinner."

Edward grinned. He was already beginning to like Martha Randall.

"What else did she say?"

"Carrie has been working for Analee Adler for years as her secretary, but the woman doesn't appreciate anything Carrie does."

"Typical mother."

Rafferty shook his head. "I don't think so. She offered some details that make me think that Carrie might be ghosting for Analee Adler."

"What details?"

"She talked about the way Carrie did most of her writing on a laptop in her apartment. Oftentimes, she would complete an entire manuscript while Ms. Adler was out of town—with no communication at all from her employer. More than that, the original notes, outlines and snatches of scenes are in Carrie's handwriting. Mrs. Randall also confessed to overhearing a conversation between Carrie and Ms. Adler, during which the author all but admitted that Carrie was the one responsible for writing the Princess Anushka novels."

Edward stared at Rafferty in disbelief. "Do our people at the publishing house know about this?"

"I made a point to call Analee's editor and have her check into the allegations. But—" he sucked in a breath "—all the evidence seems to be stacking up in Carrie's direction."

"But why would she ghost the books all this time without a word? The Princess Anushka novels are smash hits."

"Martha believes that Carrie receives a portion of the royalties. The money is good—better than Carrie could get anywhere else. Added to that is her evident enjoyment for the characters she has developed. Although she could probably sell her own work, she wishes to spin stories involving Anushka and Boris."

Edward mulled over the snatches of Carrie's biography that he been given so far. "So when Carrie hit her head, she automatically regressed to a fictional character that she herself helped develop."

"Exactly."

"So her only reason for being on the launch and coming to Babcock Island..."

"Was to deliver Analee Adler's luggage."

"And jewelry," Edward added.

"Yes, sir." He consulted his notes again. "Mrs. Randall also stated that Carrie has amassed a sizable nest egg. She fears that her daughter means to use it to exact some sort of revenge from Greg Chaney." Rafferty grinned. "I was pleased to inform Mrs. Randall that Greg Chaney is already serving concurrent sentences for fraud and larceny and won't be eligible for parole for more than fifteen years."

Edward nodded to show he understood, even as his brain raced to absorb the mountain of information he'd received.

"There is one more thing, sir," Rafferty admitted, somewhat reluctantly. "I'm afraid Mrs. Randall has her own means of obtaining the information she requires. I was…forced to relate to her that you had a steady job, few vices and a gentlemanly upbringing.'' He tore the last sheet out of his notebook. ''This is her number. She wants to talk to you. Immediately.''

Edward numbly took the sheet of paper.

Touching his fingertips to his forehead in a mocking salute, Rafferty said, ''I'm still trying to reach Ms. Adler—just as a precaution. I'll let you know when anything new turns up.''

''Thanks, Rafferty,'' Edward murmured. Then he stared down at the numbers scrawled on the paper.

Mrs. Randall wanted to talk to him? Personally?

Why did such a fact make Edward's involvement with Anush—Carrie Randall—seem all that much more real?

Chapter Fourteen

Edward spent two hours on the phone with Mrs. Randall, then another twenty minutes with Mr. Randall, after he discovered who his wife had been talking to most of the afternoon.

At first, the conversation was stilted. Mrs. Randall had been concerned about her daughter's health, but as Edward continued to talk, she began to relax, then to carry the dialogue herself—informing Edward of childhood scrapes and adolescent pranks and giving a full account of everything that had occurred to her daughter in the past ten years.

Through it all, Edward began to see that Carrie Randall and Anushka were incredibly similar. Carrie was daring, artistic and passionate. She loved deeply and lived life to its fullest. Being prone to seasickness had kept her away from the water, but she'd skydived, raced an Indy 500 car, competed in equestrian events and catered. She'd had jobs as a belly dancer, a disc jockey and a librarian. But her one true vocation had occurred when she became

Analee's assistant and was introduced to Anushka and Boris.

By the time Edward hung up the phone, he felt as if he'd known the real Carrie Randall all his life. She was impulsive, spontaneous, and sensitive.

Just the kind of woman who appealed to him.

Even though he'd never known such a fact before.

When he finally managed to pry himself away from the phone, a glance at his watch revealed that he'd been gone far too long to offer a chat with Rafferty as an excuse for his tardiness, so he quickly punched Captain Hobbs's number instead.

"Yes."

"Hobbs, I've got a new wrinkle for that whodunit you've been writing."

"Oh?"

"Yes, I think that you should arrange for Dickerson's death to be a sham."

"Really?"

"Mmm. I think that over the course of next week's activities, it should be revealed that Dickerson is Princess Anushka's long-lost cousin."

"What?"

"Since our princess may recover her senses at any time, we'll need someone to carry on the story."

There was no response from Captain Hobbs.

"Due to the butler's death, arrange for Dickerson's twin to appear to collect the body."

"Uh-huh," Hobbs offered, but it was clear he was confused.

"Masquerading as Dickerson's debonair twin brother, Dickerson can then investigate the infiltration of MEOW."

"Meow?"

"A dastardly band of cat burglars."

"I think I'd better write this down." There was a muffled noise, and then the man mumbled, "Dickerson isn't dead. Comes back as Dickerson's twin—an evil twin, sir?"

"Sure. Go ahead."

Hobbs snickered.

"Masquerading as his own evil twin, Dax—"

"Dax?"

"I like the sound of the name, don't you?"

"It works for me."

"Anyway, masquerading as Dax, he woos Ethel for information concerning MEOW."

"How much wooing?"

"As much as you think you can get away with before Dickerson has both our heads."

"Okeydokey."

"Dax believes that Ethel is part of the plot, but by the end of the week, he uncovers that Doc Little is the ringleader of MEOW."

"Doc Little?"

"I think it's a nice twist. Don't you?"

"He'll be furious at being included in the acting."

"I'm counting on it."

Hobbs chortled. "So I'll lead the guests on a merry chase until they discover that all of the events they've witnessed are not crimes of passion..."

"But one man's driving greed and his attempt to steal the Czarina's jewels."

"Which Czarina?"

"Alexandra."

"Okay, fine." There was the sound of a pencil scratching furiously against paper. "Where will we obtain these jewels? They'll need to be seen."

"I'll have Princess Anushka wear something tonight, and you can spread the word that the Czarina loaned them to her for this particular party."

"Sounds good to me." There was a slight pause, then: "But I thought you told me to keep things simple."

Edward grinned to himself. "That was before I realized that life itself is rarely ever simple."

"Whatever you say. In the meantime, I'd better get in touch with Dickerson. He's going to need to find an outfit worthy of someone named Dax."

"You'd better notify Ethel, as well. Perhaps she should have the night off."

"Mmm-hmm. I'll see if she can't borrow something...slinky to wear."

The two men burst out laughing at the same moment.

Edward was still grinning to himself when he disconnected the phone in the study and made his way to the portrait of his mother and father. Reaching for the latch that would release the door to the secret passageway, he paused, drawn to the expressions of mutual adoration on his parents' faces. The way their fingers were intimately woven together, despite the artist's complaints that the position wasn't nearly as attractive as having them fold their hands in their laps.

Hands.

His mother's hand.

Edward's eyes narrowed as he took in the jewelry his mother had worn. A bracelet and ring fit for a queen. Long ago, his mother had offered to pass down the significant pieces to her only son. But he'd never felt the need...

Turning on his toe, he returned to the desk.

He had one more call to make.

EDWARD HEARD the tap on the door and strode to admit Dickerson before Anush—Carrie—emerged from the bathroom.

"Did you find it?" he asked quickly.

Dickerson held out a flat velvet box. "May I offer my congratulations, sir?"

Edward's lips twitched in a sheepish smile. "You may. Let's just hope that your good wishes still hold true by the end of the evening."

Dickerson nodded. The truth of Princess Anushka's identity had already spread through the security staff and the household servants. It was comforting to know they were rooting for Edward's future.

"I...I mean, we all have every confidence in you,

sir." Dickerson's eyes twinkled. "As well as in the young lady."

"Thank you."

"You'll pardon me, though, if I don't linger." Dickerson's lips pressed together in evident pique. "It seems I'm about to be reincarnated as my own evil twin."

Edward made his expression purposely bland. "How curious."

"Boris?" Carrie called from the bathroom.

Placing a finger to his lips, Dickerson withdrew.

Before Edward could close the door, Carrie emerged, her body clad in buttercup yellow silk lingerie. Her hair had been coiffed close to her head in finger waves, and her makeup for the evening made her eyes look even larger and lovelier.

"Who was that at the door?" she inquired.

"A deliveryman."

Her carefully penciled brows lifted. "A deliveryman? On an island?"

"It's amazing what they'll do if you tip them well."

She grinned at him and sauntered to the armoire. The gown she had chosen was of a much later period than those she'd worn so far, Edward realized as he watched her slip into the pale bias-cut evening gown, then drape a bolero fashioned entirely of ostrich plumes over her shoulders and the plunging V of flesh exposed in the back.

After his crash course in fashion over the past

few days, he guessed the gown had been constructed in the mid-thirties by...

"Molyneux?" he inquired.

"Yes." She seemed inordinately pleased with his correct assumption. "He calls it a 'Japanese' gown."

Edward didn't see a trace of a Japanese element to the design, save for the narrow slit skirt and the train that flowed from her body on all sides.

"It's beautiful."

He'd really meant to say that *she* was beautiful, and he knew by the pinkening of her cheeks that she had interpreted his remark correctly.

"Thank you."

"I'll just pick out a bauble from one of the Czarina's things. Then I'll be right with you."

As she disappeared into the bathroom to retrieve the case she'd hung to drain over the bathtub, Edward cursed himself for not jumping at the perfect opening Carrie had given him.

Bauble? My dear, why don't you wear this little nothing? It has a funny story behind it.

Not a funny story, a romantic story. A sensitive story.

Damn. He'd never thought talking to a woman could be so nerve-racking.

But then, he'd never thought he would invite a woman who didn't know her real name to stay on his island and allow him to court her once she'd recovered. They would both need a chance to learn more about each other, to fall in love with Edward and Carrie, not Anushka and Boris.

"Boris! Come here!"

At her strident tone, Edward set the box on the back of the settee and hurried into the bathroom, sure that some new disaster had struck the infamous "Princess Anushka."

But as he burst into the room, he heard her begin to laugh.

"What is it?" he asked, almost afraid to see why she was hunched over the rim of the bathtub.

"See for yourself."

She stood then, revealing the Czarina's jewelry case—or Analee Adler's, if the truth be known. Carrie had spread a towel over the porcelain, then opened the globe to reveal its contents.

At first glance, Edward couldn't see the cause for Carrie's amusement. Inside, the case was salt-stained and dirty, and the jewelry peeling…

Peeling?

Astonished, he gazed at Carrie. "They're fake?"

She giggled. "Every one of them."

"So our diving expedition was completely…"

"Unnecessary," she finished.

Still laughing, she brushed past him and retrieved her elbow-length gloves for the evening. Grasping them in one hand, she gathered the feathered bag that held her lipstick and compact. "Although I suppose the word *unnecessary* is a bit harsh. The case itself is quite valuable, and it was imperative that we know whether or not MEOW had already retrieved it.''

Her face radiated with her sense of accomplishment. ''And I really enjoyed the dive. I feel much more…peaceful when I think of large bodies of water, for some reason. Perhaps because I know what lies beneath the surface now.''

When Edward followed her, she straightened his bow tie, then took his arm.

''Are you sure we have to make an appearance?'' he asked, suddenly loath to join the rest of the guests.

''Yes. Otherwise, there will be talk.''

''I don't care.''

''You should.''

He sighed, knowing that Carrie wouldn't change her mind. Going for broke, he offered hastily, ''Then perhaps you would at least consent to wearing these as your 'baubles' for the evening.''

Edward took the velvet box from the settee and opened the lid. Inside lay a curious ring made of gold and diamonds, which had been fashioned to resemble a thick band of woven wheat. The bracelet, similarly designed, sparkled with more diamond baguettes, as well as tiny opals that nestled inside the beards to resemble kernels of grain.

He noted the way Carrie held her breath.

She lifted a finger to touch them, then stroked the feathered fronds on the tassels of wheat.

''How unusual,'' she breathed.

He hoped such a comment meant she didn't find the pieces odd.

"Before you agree to wear them," Edward said quickly, "you need to know the story behind them."

She nodded, but her attention still remained on the pieces of jewelry.

"My father was a very wealthy man."

When she would have interrupted, he motioned for her to remain still. He had already conferred with the "Anushka experts" on the island, and knew that no mention of Boris's parents had ever been made. Therefore, he felt safe in the slight deviation from Boris's role in the Anushka novels.

"When he went to school, my father grew tired of the way women followed him like bees. He could never be sure if he was loved for himself, or his fortune. So one summer, he took a job as a farmhand. He altered his name and vowed to use the time to discover what he really wanted from life, love, and the future."

Carrie was listening intently and had showed no signs of trauma, so he continued.

"Once there, he met the most beautiful girl he had ever encountered, and he knew in an instant that he had met the woman he wanted to marry."

She sighed. "How romantic."

"Ah, but I've only just begun." He stepped closer. "Despite the fact that my father had fallen hopelessly in love with the farmer's daughter, he still feared that once he told her the truth about himself, she would begin to care for him for all the wrong reasons. Therefore, after a church dance, when he could no longer treat her with indifference, he fashioned a ring from three pieces of wheat.

"As he put the band on her finger, my father said that, if he could, he would offer her the world. Since that wasn't possible, he would give her a symbol of his intentions instead. Just as the wheat crop symbolized life to those who cultivated it, sold it and eventually ate it, my father promised my mother a life of happiness if she would allow him to woo her properly and win her heart."

Carrie looked up at him, her eyes bright. "You're going to make me cry, Boris."

His heart was pounding as he took the ring and the bracelet from their beds.

"My mother called her little band of wheat her 'promise ring.' She kept the band in a special box beneath her bed so that she could dream of him each night."

"She loved him, too?"

"From the moment he entered her house and made his way to the dinner table."

"Why haven't you told me this before?"

Ignoring that question for the time being, Edward continued, "On the day my mother and father were to be married, she insisted that her promise ring be slipped onto her finger beside the much more elaborate and expensive wedding set my father had made for her."

"He'd told her he was rich?"

"Yes. He'd realized soon enough that my mother loved him for who he was, not what he was."

"Did he slip the wheat on her finger during the ceremony as she wanted?"

"No."

"No?" she demanded, plainly distressed. "Why not?"

"The mice had chewed a hole in the box and eaten the wheat."

At that instant, Carrie's face mirrored the same horror his mother's always had when she told the story.

"My mother cried and cried and could not be consoled. Breaking with tradition, which stated the groom should never see the bride before the wedding, my father made a trip to the wheat field. Then, climbing the trellis to her bedroom window, he slipped inside, held her, comforted her, then presented her with a new ring and a new promise—for a life together, for all the happily-ever-afters promised in fairy tales."

He rolled the golden ring in his fingers, studying the brilliant facets.

"When I was born a year later, my father presented her with these. He wanted to make sure there would be no more problems with mice, my mother's promise ring, and the future of his new little family."

Edward caught Carrie's gaze and was touched by the tears that glittered there. "My mother offered them to me several years ago. For that time when I wished to ask a woman to let me woo her properly.''

Carrie bit her lip.

"Will you?" he asked, the words so soft and husky, he wondered if she'd heard him. But more than that, he wondered if she understood that—in his own disjointed way—he was trying to ask her to look upon him as something more than a friend, bodyguard or thwarted lover. He was asking her to learn to love him as a man who was considering a future for them both. Together.

Wordlessly, she nodded, her eyes bright. Happy tears, he hoped.

Gently, he slid the ring over her engagement finger, then looped the bracelet around her wrist. "I was told you liked opals."

"By whom?"

"Your mother."

She made no overt reaction to the tidbit gathered from her real life, and he took comfort in the fact. Perhaps she *was* ready to leave Anushka behind.

Tonight.

When they were alone.

Edward brought the ring to his lips and kissed her finger.

"You understand that the ring is only a symbol of my intentions? At any time, you're free to give it back."

She nodded.

"And you know I'm toying with the idea of a

future together—no matter what surprises the next few days might bring.''

Her head dipped again, and then she stared up at him with wide, disbelieving eyes.

''I want a chance to get to know the real you— no secrets, no facades. And I hope you'll learn as much about me.''

''Why?'' she asked in a choked voice.

''Because the first time we met, our souls touched. A man would be a fool to let circumstance get in the way of such magic.''

Again, she indicated that she understood by offering him a crooked, silly smile. Ducking her head, she studied the ring.

Carrie half sobbed, half implored. ''No more, Boris, or I'll cry and my makeup will run.'' But her protest was a sham, and they both knew it.

Pulling Carrie into his embrace, Edward kissed her with all the wonder and joy this woman had brought to him in a mere handful of days. There was still so much to worry about. Carrie's memory *would* return—soon, he sensed. He'd already seen so many signs of Anushka's facade dropping away. He had no guarantees that Carrie Randall would fall in love with him—or that his own fledgling emotions wouldn't alter once Anushka was completely banished. None at all.

But he couldn't think of such things now. He had this night—and he had the time they'd already shared together—to help him believe that miracles could really happen. The frog she'd once accused him of being could transform into a prince. And the princess...

Well, maybe she would discover that she had an affinity with former frogs.

Slowly, reluctantly, he released Carrie and allowed her to settle her heels on the floor again. Then, indulgently, he wiped away the moisture that trembled at her lashes.

"How long do we have to stay?" he whispered.

"Just until the first dance?"

Her words emerged as a question, not an order.

Chuckling, he covered the hand that rested on his forearm. The ring pressed pleasantly into his flesh.

"Come along, then. I already hear the band warming up."

Chapter Fifteen

For the first time, Boris led her through the main hall and down the winding staircase to the front foyer. With each step they took, she felt lighter and lighter—as if she could fly from the mere joy of the moment.

He loved her.

She knew he did, even if he hadn't said the words.

When he drew her into the ballroom and swept her onto the dance floor, she did not resist. Heaven for her was in this man's arms, and nothing—*nothing*—could destroy the moment. At long last, she'd found a man who could truly understand her. He wouldn't use her the way Greg had done…

Greg? The pretty boy?

He'd never treated her with such gallantry. Instead, he'd manipulated her emotions and showered her with flattery and romance. Not until later had she realized that his emotions were hollow and the flowers and gifts an attempt to manipulate her. She'd been a fool to agree to marry him.

Her brow puckered, and the pounding in her head increased.

Marry? She'd never been engaged before. Anushka wouldn't tie herself down to...down to...

A rustle of voices began in the far corner of the room and flowed through to the double doors of the terrace. A man stood silhouetted in the archway. A man who looked very much like...

"I've come to demand vengeance for my brother's death!" he shouted.

Please, she thought with a touch of disbelief. *Vengeance?* The word sounded like something from a historical novel.

Or a spy thriller.

The man strode into the room, and she was relieved when her companion stopped dancing. The room felt like it was unaccountably close in around her, and tiny pricks of light kept washing in front of her gaze.

"Where is the person responsible? I demand that—"

A host of muffled shouts drowned out the man's words—then came a woman's shrill voice, a squeal of displeasure.

"Damn it, man! Unhand me! I've told you over and over that I have an invitation to this event. So what if it wasn't delivered to me personally? Mr. Babcock will insist on my attendance at his party. After all, I've come to inform Mr. Babcock of an impostor in his midst."

The strident voice grew louder. Even the man so similar to Dickerson turned to look.

A chill rushed through her body. She touched a finger to her head as the scene in front of her tipped and swayed.

Boris's hands tightened on her waist.

From outside, deep voices rose in confusion.

"You can't barge in—"

"Ow!"

"Grab her!"

Seconds later, a tall, rawboned woman darted into the ballroom. Skidding to a halt, she began to search the gathering, her lips puckering into a thin slash of fury. Then her gaze fell on Anushka and Boris, beneath the center chandelier.

"That woman!" the intruder proclaimed, her leopard-print cape swirling around her shoulders as she lifted a finger to point in their direction. She prowled forward, her sequined boots glittering, her white-blond hair gleaming in the low lights.

The swirling sensation was growing more insistent. So much so that Boris had to take her weight to keep her from falling. The bright spots were growing wider, more insistent, crowding out her vision.

"She's no guest," the intruder announced in a haughty tone. "She's my *secretary*. A nothing. A nobody."

The room seemed to jump, swirl. Carrie blinked as Analee approached. The woman's lips narrowed into a slash of displeasure, and in an instant, the past few days melted away and Carrie's true self burst to the fore.

Analee Adler has returned from Rome and she'll be wanting her jewelry.

Of all the thoughts to take hold, it was the first. Then, swiftly on its heels, came the memory of the accident and those confusing moments when Carrie had awakened to find herself being cradled in the arms of a strange man. A man she had mistaken for a character from the novels she wrote.

Boris?

Blearily she stared up at her companion. From some point far removed from the situation, she heard him murmur, ''Anushka?''

But she wasn't Anushka. Anushka wasn't real. She was the stuff of dreams. Carrie's dreams. Carrie's writing.

And this man wasn't Boris.

He was a stranger.

She gazed up at him in bewilderment, knowing that she'd kissed him, caressed him. She'd spoken to him as if he were her lackey—and all the while he'd played along.

Mortified, Carrie remembered all she'd done and said over the past few days. And now, when she was still drawn to this man, still felt safe in his arms, she realized she didn't even know his name.

Unwillingly, she looked down at her hand, focusing on the golden ring, the sparkling bracelet. The tragedy of the moment struck her to the core.

It had all been a game.

A fantasy.

None of it had been real.

A choked cry burst from her lips. Her stomach roiled as if she were once again on the launch, the sun beating down on her head, the gold jewelry box clutched in her hands. She could remember standing, the sudden bump from the pier...

Then her world faded into darkness.

"CATCH HER!"

Edward didn't need Dickerson's instinctive warning. He was already sweeping Carrie into his arms and carrying her through the sea of guests.

"Damn it, where is Babcock?" Analee exclaimed in disgust as the attention was drawn away from her. Planting her hands on her hips, she scanned the astonished guests' faces. "I demand he be fetched at once. *He'll* listen to me. He'll appreciate the fact that I've come to relieve him of this...gate-crasher."

Edward felt Carrie stir in his arms. He was eager to carry her somewhere private, but Analee's shrill tone caused him to pause and turn to face the woman who had forced Carrie to face her true self—perhaps damaging her recovery in the process.

After all that he, Dickerson, Doc Little and Hobbs had done to protect her mind from being wrenched out of its cocoon, this woman had purposely stomped into Edward's home, intent on hurting Carrie.

"Well?" Analee demanded. "Get Mr. Babcock.

Go on, get him! I promise he'll be thankful to see me.''

"I'm afraid you're mistaken.''

Edward's voice boomed through the room, and he fought to hold on to the tight rein on his temper.

Carrie stirred against him, her eyes fluttering.

"This woman is here at my invitation,'' he proclaimed loudly.

Doc Little and Dickerson exchanged glances, and Edward was aware that his voice held the razor-sharp edge he used only when severely provoked.

Analee sniffed. "*Your* invitation? You've got to be joking.''

Carrie had lifted her head now and was making a weak attempt to stand on her own, but Edward held her tight.

"I can assure you, Ms. Adler, that I am not joking.''

Analee studied him distastefully. "And just *who* are *you?*''

His lips tilted in a slow, rich smile. "*I* am Edward Remington Babcock.''

Analee grew pale, her mouth opening and closing like a starved fish. Then, one foot inched behind the other and she began to curtsy, as if Edward were visiting royalty.

Around the room, guests began to whisper and gasp, but Edward had eyes for no one but the woman in his arms. Carrie regarded him with such a mixture of anguish and despair that he knew he had to take her somewhere private and explain how they'd both arrived at this point.

Carrie quickly looked around her, and Edward knew she noted how none of the servants appeared the least bit surprised by the pronouncement. Then he saw her cringe, and he could all but read her thoughts. She was sure that Edward Babcock—a man who had kept his identity a secret more than thirty years—would hate her for forcing him to reveal his true name.

Sobbing, Carrie did her best to pull free, but he held her fast, willing her to look in his eyes and see the same emotions that had been there when he gave her his mother's promise jewelry.

Nothing had changed.

He still had great hope for the future.

He still believed that with time their relationship would grow, not shatter.

"Don't let a slight change in names alter what we have together, Carrie," he murmured for her ears alone.

Tears fell down her cheeks.

"An accident may have brought you to me. Your recovery may have allowed us to spend time together. But I can assure you, I *do* still wish to court you. Call it love at first sight. The phenomenon runs in my family."

She trembled, biting her lip as if she still didn't believe him.

"We'll have plenty of time to get to know one

another properly—our true selves—if you'll only take a chance on me.''

The tears flowed more quickly now, and Carrie threw her arms around his neck.

He held her close, crushing her to him.

''Take a chance on me,'' he repeated close to her ear.

''What's going on in here?'' a deep voice grumbled, and Edward started, then began to laugh.

''Somehow, I knew they wouldn't wait until morning.''

''They?'' Carrie repeated.

Setting Carrie on her feet, Edward pulled her against him, her back to his chest, and wrapped his arms around her waist. Bending, he rested his chin on her shoulder and whispered next to her ear, ''After tracking their movements halfway across the globe, I finally located my parents in Manhattan last night. They were resting from their recent trip when I managed to get them on the phone. The moment I asked about the promise jewelry, they insisted I give them the details of the woman I'd met.''

He felt her strength falter as she whispered, ''Oh, no.''

Edward laughed and swept her into his arms. ''Faint,'' he ordered.

''What?''

''Pretend you're Anushka and I'm Boris and this is our first encounter. Then faint.''

In an instant, she went lax in his arms.

Epilogue

Midnight had come and gone when Carrie flung herself on the bed and kicked off her satin pumps. Gazing up at the ceiling, she marveled at how much could change in such a short amount of time. In one mere month, she'd lost her identity, met a marvelous man, lived out a fantasy, recovered her past, been properly wooed, become engaged, and been welcomed into one of the wealthiest families in the world.

Now, she was married.

Mrs. Edward Remington Babcock.

And all because of a little bump on the head.

Closing her eyes in delight, she recalled the days spent with Edward on his island—the picnics, the scuba diving, the long evenings in front of the fire. But most of all, she remembered the long talks they'd shared, the unveiling of their souls. To their mutual delight, such information had only brought them closer. So much so that they'd begun to realize that there was only a minute difference between

Anushka and Boris's relationship and that shared by Carrie and Edward.

Her lips tilted in a smug grin.

One of those differences would soon be under-scored once and for all. Tonight was their wedding night. Edward's parents were no longer on the is-land to serve as unwitting chaperons. Doc Little had gone to visit his grandchildren. Rafferty and the se-curity team were roaming the beaches to discourage paparazzi. And Dickerson, surprisingly enough, had invited Ethel to accompany him on a three-day bus tour of the Canadian coast.

"What are you thinking?"

"How lovely the upper sitting room is since you painted it red."

"Liar."

She smiled when Edward approached the bed, his fingers plucking at his tie.

"Then perhaps I was pondering how lucky I am."

He tried not to grin, but she noted his pleasure.

"I hope my parents didn't overwhelm you with their insistence on accompanying us nearly every minute of the day. They're from an earlier genera-tion."

"I think their concern for my virtue is sweet."

He grimaced. "They never thought I'd marry at all. I'm sure they wanted to do everything in their power to keep you from changing your mind."

She touched the band of her ring with her thumb. This time, with her mother-in-law's approval, the promise ring had become part of Carrie's wedding set.

"Your parents are wonderful. Not at all what I would have expected from such a wealthy couple."

Edward snorted. "What *did* you expect?"

"People more like Analee."

He grimaced. "That woman is a menace. No wonder you were afraid she'd mount your head on her wall next to the water buffalo."

She giggled. "She's afraid of you, Edward. I hope you realized that fact."

"I don't know why you insisted on inviting her to the wedding," he grumbled.

Carrie grinned mischievously. "Call it my own poetic justice. Of course, at the time, I didn't realize how much you terrified her."

"She should be terrified. She's treated you very shabbily."

Carrie waved that remark away, enjoying the way the light glittered from her ring and cast rainbows over the antique satin wedding gown she wore. Edward had purchased the twenties ensemble from the same shop in Atlanta that had provided him with his first real clue toward her identity. When she opened the box, he'd uttered, "Worth," as if he were offering Boris's approval, as well.

"I don't know how you can be civil with Analee after the way she used you, Carrie."

She wrenched her mind back to the conversation at hand. "It was my own fault. I knew what Analee was doing was wrong. I never should have agreed to completely write her books without insisting on partial credit. But at the time, I was feeling very angry and blue. Neither of those emotions leads to clear thinking.''

"How do you feel now?" Edward asked as his hands reached for the studs of his shirt.

She watched as he revealed the broad planes of his chest and the corrugated muscles of his stomach. How long had it been since she had free rein of that warm skin?

Forever.

She stretched like a cat. "Right now, I feel wonderful.''

"No regrets?''

"None.''

He threw his shirt on a nearby chair. "You certainly livened up my gala, Miss Randall. Dickerson informed me we made over two-million dollars with the fund-raiser.''

She giggled, remembering a twitterpated Mrs. Peery, the case of salt-eaten jewelry, and her chastened employer.

"It was fun, wasn't it?''

His expression grew positively wicked. "Not as fun as it could have been. Not as fun as the next few hours will be.''

"Whatever do you mean?" she asked coyly.

But she knew exactly what he intended. After all, they were alone in the house, wedding rings graced their fingers, and the night could hold only one possible conclusion to make the day perfectly complete.

His finely tailored trousers hung low on his hips as Edward braced a knee on the mattress and planted his hands on either side of her head.

"I've been giving the matter a good deal of thought, and I've decided that the time has long since passed for us to move to the next stage of our relationship."

"Oh, really?" Her saucy reply was barely a whisper. A very uneven and garbled whisper.

Her hands slid up his chest, and she reveled in his quick intake of breath.

He grabbed her hand and placed a kiss in her palm. Then, waggling his brows suggestively, he offered, "What do you say you and I...you know."

Her laughter caught in her throat as a pang of desire skittered through her body. She loved this man, heart and soul, just as she knew he loved her.

"Mmm. I'd like that very much."

"You're sure?"

She wrapped her arms around his neck. "Very sure," she purred, pulling him down for her kiss. "I might even find a way for Boris to be cured, so that Princess Anushka can be relieved of her misery, as well."

He groaned, settling his weight upon her. "Your fans would heartily approve." The words were fraught with barely controlled passion as he kissed her cheek, her jaw, then nipped her ear. "Especially this fan."

She sighed in pleasure, her hands clinging to the

strong muscles of his back as her own desire threatened to inundate her.

"But this time," Edward murmured when he finally traversed the distance to her lips. "This time, you'll write about Anushka and Boris under your own name. I insist."

"Can you do that?" she teased, business the last thing on her mind.

"Yes. I can. After all, I'm Edward Remington Babcock."

"Your anonymity is shattered."

"Good riddance."

"You might not think so when you leave the island and the paparazzi begin trailing you."

"Somehow, I think they'll be more interested in you than in me."

"Then maybe we should plan to spend the next few months here in this house," she suggested.

"Perhaps you're right."

She chuckled at his no-nonsense tone, but her mirth soon dissolved in a wave of sheer pleasure as Edward's hand caressed her breast through the thin fabric of her gown.

"Enough talking, Edward," she said with a sigh, pulling him closer to kiss him, then kissing him again.

"There's still your mother to call," he offered, but she knew he wasn't serious. "We told her we'd check to make sure they got home safely."

"She'd kill us both if we called after ten," she

said with utmost sincerity, her hands roaming the crease of his spine.

"Heaven knows, I wouldn't want to offend my in-laws," Edward murmured against her throat.

Carrie gasped, barely managing to say, "That's probably a wise decision."

"Especially since we'll someday have babies for them to tend while—"

She pulled his lips to hers, whispering, "Right now, I don't care about any of that. Right now, all I want is you, a soft bed and…"

"You know," he finished, his voice filled with passion.

"Mmm. Yes, I do."

EVER HAD ONE OF THOSE DAYS?

TO DO:

- ☑ at the supermarket buying two dozen muffins that your son just remembered to tell you he needed for the school treat, you realize you left your wallet at home

- ☑ at work just as you're going into the big meeting, you discover your son took your presentation to school, and you have his hand-drawn superhero comic book

- ☑ your mother-in-law calls to say she's coming for a month-long visit

- ☑ finally at the end of a long and exasperating day, you escape from it all with an entertaining, humorous and always romantic Love & Laughter book!

ENJOY
LOVE & LAUGHTER™
EVERY DAY!

For a preview, turn the page....

*Here's a sneak peek at
Carrie Alexander's THE AMOROUS HEIRESS
Available September 1997...*

"YOU'RE A VERY popular lady," Jed Kelley observed as Augustina closed the door on her suitors.

She waved a hand. "Just two of a dozen." Technically true since her grandmother had put her on the open market. "You're not afraid of a little competition, are you?"

"Competition?" He looked puzzled. "I thought the position was mine."

Augustina shook her head, smiling coyly. "You didn't think Grandmother was the final arbiter of the decision, did you? I say a trial period is in order." No matter that Jed Kelley had miraculously passed Grandmother's muster, Augustina felt the need for a little propriety. But, on the other hand, she could be married before the summer was out and be free as a bird, with the added bonus of a husband it wouldn't be all that difficult to learn to love.

She got up the courage to reach for his hand, and then just like that, she—Miss Gussy Gutless Fairchild—was holding Jed Kelley's hand. He looked down at their linked hands. "Of course, you don't really know what sort of work I can do, do you?"

A funny way to put it, she thought absently, cradling his callused hand between both of her own. "We can get to know each other, and then, if that works out..." she murmured. *Wow.* If she'd known what this arranged marriage thing was all about, she'd have been a supporter of Grandmother's campaign from the start!

"Are you a palm reader?" Jed asked gruffly. His voice was as raspy as sandpaper and it was rubbing her all the right ways, but the question flustered her. She dropped his hand.

"I'm sorry."

"No problem," he said, "as long as I'm hired."

"Hired!" she scoffed. "What a way of putting it!"

Jed folded his arms across his chest. "So we're back to the trial period."

"Yes." Augustina frowned and her gaze dropped to his work boots. Okay, so he wasn't as well off as the majority of her suitors, but really, did he think she was going to *pay* him to marry her?

"Fine, then." He flipped her a wave and, speechless, she watched him leave. She was trembling all over like a malaria victim in a snowstorm, shot with hot charges and cold shivers until her brain was numb. This couldn't be true. Fantasy men didn't happen to nice girls like her.

"Augustina?"

Her grandmother's voice intruded on Gussy's privacy. "Ahh. There you are. I see you met the new gardener?"